In the Land of the Chalice Maker

T.J. CAHILL

ISBN 1450547230

EAN-139781450547239

ACKNOWLEDGEMENTS

A novelist writes the story alone but would never be able to get it in print without the help of a few good people along the way.

Jeffery Etter steered me through the final layout design, edit and formatting process when I was still looking for an ink well, quill and parchment paper to publish on. His skills were invaluable and I still don't know how he does what he does, but I am very grateful that he does.

Most importantly, I want to thank my dear friend Eileen Rosenberger who has always encouraged me to write, write and write. So I did. She is an absolute dream of a friend and no one could ever ask for a better one.

Rest assured, there will be more novels on the way!

DEDICATION

This book is dedicated to my paternal great-grandfather, J.T. Cahill, a good man and a salt-of-the-earth laborer who could barely write his own name when he emmigrated from Ireland to America in 1880 as a young man. I think he would take great pride in knowing that his great-grandson turned out to be a writer.

Part One

Chapter One

To an outsider, it seemed like a terribly unusual land — for its place and time, that is. It was thought to be a quiet land, but also known to be full of surprises. It was quite a beautiful land — especially the forest. To be sure, it had its share of legends and myths and some even carried a reknown beyond its invisible borders. For instance, magic was rarely spoken of and power, if abused, had unmentionable consequences. But, in similar fashion to other unnamed lands, fish were caught in nets and carnivores brought down with arrows. It was nearly like other places save for one glorious herald: this place was the Land of the Chalice Maker. It carried this solitary imprimatur with pride to define its uniqueness and call attention to its inhabitants. Even though everyone knew that, in truth, the land was every bit as powerful as it was magical; most of its inhabitants were delighted by the magic but afraid of the power. In the odd instance, there were some who were afraid of both. Chalice Makers knew about both and cared about neither. In this land, Chalice Makers were special. It was not so much a gift that one was born with, but one that was bestowed upon them. One young, brave inhabitant was about to learn just how very special the Land of the Chalice Maker could be. His odyssey was just beginning.

Palryma, son of Bestra and Merrilyee, was chosen to be a chalice maker when he was 23 years old. That was rather a late age to be chosen especially since the newly chosen one carries with him, by legend and decree, the cumulative age of all the previous chalice makers in his line. To his friends, Palryma was 23 years old but to the gifted line of chalice makers gone before him, he was 8,265 years old. He had a lot to live up to.

The wizened old chalice makers who had long since slipped their mortal coils also took their sweet time in deciding just exactly who they wanted to join their lines. Aside from Palryma, there were presently only two other chalice makers in the land. One was Great Ben who had been making chalices long before Palryma was born and whom most people in the land thought might be well over 15,000 years old. His work was exquisite and much sought after. It was rumored that one of his early chalices was in the Castle of Hurrah III and was used at the wedding of his father Hurrah II. No one alive in the land had ever seen it and no one ever was invited inside the castle. So, it remained a rumor.

The day that the gift of chalice making was bestowed upon Palryma he was innocently walking through the wet fields no more than a mile from his home in Goosra, a quiet place, but the most important village in the land. He had wood for the fire and two big Shatoo birds he hunted down for a special feast that evening for his parents. They were wedded 24 years on that very day and the Shatoo birds were a lucky catch, as they were not often seen in the wet fields. "A very fine addition for my parents wedding celebration," thought Palmyra as he whistled his favorite walking songs. "These beautiful birds will make the table look as good as anything in the Castle of Hurrah III!" The evening was set to be spent in merriment among friends around a nice warm fire listening to tales of the land.

Nearing the edge of the wet fields, Palryma felt an uncharacteristic need to sit himself down on one of the big rocks that separated the fields from the main dirt road leading towards Goosra. He felt his sturdy legs weaken and thought he just might have stood in the wet fields too long while looking for something special to bring home. All his young life he ignored the Legend of the Wet Fields — something that made him a fearless hunter by the time he was but 13 years old. Legend had it that when anyone stayed too long in the wet fields the wetness seeped into their boots and from there it rapidly sped up the inside of the legs making it nearly impossible to walk or even lift a leg. Many a hunter in the land was known to have died from staying in the wet fields for too long a time — some got the wetness inside their legs when they were too far from the edge of the fields and never made it out.

Only once before had Palryma been close to falling prey to the Legend of the Wet Fields. He was 17 and had just hunted down the biggest Simeeore boar he had ever seen. It was so big that it held enough meat on its bones to feed the entire village of Goosra. He had great difficulty dragging it out of the wet fields and had to use every ounce of his considerable strength to get it to the main road. He was exhausted and could hardly lift his legs to kick the heavy boar over the rocks lining the edge. But he succeeded and rested for a moment after the animal rolled onto the main road. It was in that moment that Palryma nearly died. It was after he rested his weary head in his arms and propped himself up against the rocks that he could feel the wetness seeping into the soles of his boots. Had he waited a second longer he would have died in the wet fields like many average hunters in the land. But there was nothing average about Palryma. He quickly wrapped his muscled arms around the lowest rock in the fence and began to use all the mighty force of his upper torso to pull his limping legs away from the wetness. He pulled on the rocks for dear life, bloodying his fingers in the process, and crawled up just high enough to push himself with full force out of the wet fields, tumbling head first onto the main road.

"Sweet Lenora-ga in heaven but that was close!" he exclaimed, "I must watch myself next time." He knew as surely as he had just made it out of the wet fields that there would certainly be a next time. Palryma was a fearless hunter and the best hunting in the land was in the wet fields. "Maybe next time," he smiled. "I won't try to feed the whole village!" But feed them he did on that night. The villagers spotted Palryma dragging the big dead beast down the road and word spread more rapidly than the news of the death of Hurrah II that there would be a big, fine feast in Goosra that night. And the feast was a memorable one indeed. Boar is a delicacy throughout the land and ones as huge as the one Palryma hunted down in Goosra had only ever been seen from the road's edge. They stood prominently in the wet fields, breathing yellow smoke as cold as mountain-top snow from their nostrils, almost daring the hunters from the village to enter and try to hunt them down. None but Palryma ever did for he was determined to destroy the myth that while a good strong hunter might survive the wet fields, no huge Simeeore boar could ever be hunted down and dragged out.

The village square was lit with the smiles of sated villagers all of whom praised the brave 17-year-old hunter. Bigger praise was saved for his parents, Bestra and Merrilyee. "You have raised the bravest lad in the land," shouted the Mayor of Goosra before he laid his sharpest knife into the cooked boar. Protocol required that the first slice be presented to Merrilyee, the second slice to Bestra and the third to Palryma himself. After that, the villagers all line up for their share and there was more than enough for seconds and thirds for all of them. Songs were whistled and sung, hands were clapped in time and dancing in the street lasted until every belly in the village was filled to capacity. The bonfire in the village square was massive and Palryma was a hero at 17 years old.

All this merriment could be seen by Hurrah III from his dark castle high atop the Dusky Hill. It was the huge bonfire that caught his eye. He sent his talking bird, Settela, down to see what was causing such commotion. Settela reported "My Lord, it is a celebration for the heroism of the young villager Palryma. He has killed a huge Simeeore boar in the wet fields and now the entire village is feasting on it."

"Damn him anyway," snarled Hurrah III. "How did he get out of those wet fields alive with that beast?"

Hurrah III saw everything from his castle perch. No one ever saw him. "That boy is being watched over. I just know it."

Watched over or not, the fact remained that the villagers loved Palryma and had done so his whole life. He was always considered to be a special child. Now, five years after the memorable village feast, five years after he challenged and beat the Legend of the Wet Fields, the handsome, 23 year-old Palryma was about to become a Chalice Maker – one of only three in the land.

"It is time now to bestow our gift on this young man," declared Batoowa, the oldest and most revered chalice maker in this revered line of masters looking down upon Palryma as he rested briefly. "We have watched him for a long while now. He shows the grace and bravery we have long sought in candidate so that our line may continue. He will stay strong and use the gift well. He loves the land."

"And most importantly, he has the true heart of a chalice maker," said Pormetah. "It is true that he may be loyal to the land. Yes. And it is true that he loves his parents. Yes. And we can see that he has no fear. Yes. But, other young boys in the land hold these traits. Not all of them have the heart of a chalice maker. Palryma has this. Yes. I want him to join our line." He roared, "Yes, I do."

His was a very important vote because Pormetah was the last hunter to be made a chalice maker in this line. By coincidence and occasion, he was also the very last to hunt down a Simeeore boar and bring it into the village of Goosra. He was but 14 years old at the time and made a vow that he would honor the presence of Hurrah the Beloved on the throne by offering the elusive beast of the wet fields to the new king. Hurrah the Beloved was the great-great-great-great grandfather of Hurrah II. On the very day he presented the massive beast to the new king, the gift of the chalice maker was bestowed upon Pormetah. He knew what beat deep inside Palryma's heart and he knew it was the true heart of a chalice maker. Pormetah knew what it was like to have that special kind of heart. From the experience of his own life, Pormetah knew exactly what it meant.

The vote was unanimous. Every chalice maker in the line seemed well pleased with this choice.

"Shall we begin?" asked Batoowa. All nodded in agreement.

"All right then." he said rubbing his hands. "Nesella," he bellowed, "are you ready!?"

"I am, Your Grace," she cried with great and bursting enthusiasm "I am most ready!"

"Then do what must be done!!!" said Batoowa as he rose to his full Chalice Maker height and clapped his hands together like thunder bolts. "DRY UP THE WET FIELDS!!!"

And so she did. With one long, powerful inhaling breath, Nesella dried them up and simultaneously captured inside of her for this brief bestowing time the Legend of the Wet Fields.

For any master in the line of chalice makers to inhale a legend of the land was a very dangerous thing to do. This was especially true for the Legend of the Wet Fields. If inhaled for too long a time, the wetness could activate itself inside the master, pull them from the line and make them forever a deadly part of the wet fields. But, Nesella's bravery was well known by all the chalice makers in the line and all knew that she was perfect for this task.

As Palryma watched in wonderment what was happening to the wet fields, he knew with keen instinct that he must jump to the rocks at the edge of the road immediately, Shatoo birds in hand, no mater how tired he was. He sensed a presence approaching but he did not realize that his fate was clearly not in his hands.

"Palryma, son of Bestra and Merrilyee, hero hunter of the village of Goosra — stand fast in the face of the Chalice Makers gone before you!!" was the deafening cry piercing his young ears.

"Rise to your height and acknowledge the magic and power of the land!"

There were thousands of violet and green colored swirls of sweet-smelling smoke surrounding Palryma and the faint, tiny tinkling of a million morning bells in the distance. "Who calls to me in this fashion? Who is it that cares to show me magic and power? I am only Palryma, a young village hunter from Goosra."

"We know who you are. We have been watching you."

A worried look etched its way onto Palryma's smooth face. An uncharacteristic furrowed brow bore itself across his fore-head. "I put to you, magical ones, that I have done nothing wrong. I bring these Shatoo birds for my parents' wedding celebration this very night. I am a good son. They will be a gift to honor them. Nothing more."

The faces of Batoowa, Pormetah, Nesella and all the rest of the chalice makers in the line began to appear in the green and violet smoke and the morning bells began to ring very loudly and with an echo that could be heard all the way down in the village. Palryma felt he was becoming dizzy from the swirling smoke and magical faces and had to steady his legs. He dared not fall off the rock upon which he stood for he saw that the wet fields had dried up. He did not know what magic caused this but cared not to test its power. "I plead my case again!" he shouted, "I am an innocent and I do no one any harm." He folded his hunter's hands in prayer and raised them to the sky. "Please tell me why you have stopped me here. Why can I not go home to my parents' wedding celebration? What do you want with a poor hunter?"

"You will become one of us," was the answer.

The words of it almost stopped Palryma's heart from beating. The answer hung in the air like rainbow colors amid the sweet sound of the million morning bells ringing.

"This cannot be true," replied Palryma "How can I, Palryma, son of Bestra and Merrilyee, become a Chalice Maker in the land?"

"Because we have decided it will be so," said Batoowa "We have decided that we will bestow the gift of chalice making upon you, my son, because you have proven yourself to be an honorable man. In you beats the heart of a chalice maker. This we know for sure."

"But when.... How.... I don't understand..." Batoowa interrupted Palryma's confusion.

"It happens NOW!!"

With that bellicose command from Batoowa, Palryma was miraculously lifted up into the blue skies of Goosra and his body was spun 'round and 'round at a dizzying speed. Pormetah grabbed his hands and shook Palryma like an old rug. Nesella turned his skin to violet, the color of his eyes..... and then back again. Every walking song he had ever whistled since he learned to whistle at the age of three came streaming out of his lips with the clarity and pitch of a master musician. Batoowa took hold of the spinning hunter and threw him like a boomerang across the land. Suddenly he was tumbling amongst the fluffy white clouds with the ease of the Shattoo birds and could see for miles and miles – past the castle of Hurrah III atop the Dusky Hill into Latima – an evil and mysterious place forbidden for anyone in the land to enter. The sound of a million bells ringing turned their notes every color of the rainbow. There was no mistaking this announcement. No one in the village of Goosra could miss it as the skies were now filled with heavenly music while little colored musical notes floated gently to the ground.

"There's to be a new chalice maker!" cried Simmee-Sammy, the village historian. He had not seen this wonderment from the skies in far too many years.

The last time was when Billora, the kindly but poor stone crusher received the gift of chalice making. His sad tale was legend in the land but especially in Goosra where his blind father still made fishing nets from the stringy marrow of the big-boned river fish. Billora heard of a cure for blindness that was suppose to be way, way behind the Dusky Hill — in fact, hundreds of miles into Latima. He had been warned many times that he must first learn the ways of a chalice maker but, against the strong advice of his guide, he did not listen. He loved his father so and wanted to use his powers as a chalice maker to bring home the cure to Goosra. One day he wandered far past the Dusky Hill in search of this cure and was never heard from again. The loneliness and sadness in the eyes of Billora's father could be seen even now. With every string of fish marrow he twisted and with each and every single net he sewed, he hoped that one day Billora would find his way back home — back to the loving arms and warm touch of his sightless father. "I never needed a cure," Pantara always told his neighbors. "But, I have always needed my son and I pray to Sweet Lenora-ga every day that he will come back to me."

As tiny musical notes dropped into the village, everyone could see now who would be the new chalice maker because all the notes bore only one word: Palryma. There was one huge collective smile from all the villagers when they saw this. Instantly they knew that the wedding celebration of Bestra and Merrilyee tonight would now be one for all the ages.

Their son was now the new chalice maker in the land.

The initiation rite now complete and the gift officially bestowed, Batoowa raised his powerful arms above his head and slowly lowered them and with that lowering, the young new chalice maker was carefully set to rest on the road just outside the wet fields.

"Exhale Nesella!!" commanded Batoowa. "The gift is now and forever properly bestowed upon our young hunter. He is now a chalice maker."

"Yes. He is the new one! Yes he is," cried Pormetah with great acclaim "Yes! And everyone in the village now knows this. Yes they do! And just in time as well! One more second of holding her breath in and our brave Nesella would have been poisoned herself. Yes she would! Your timing, as always, Batoowa was perfect. Yes it was!"

With one long powerful exhale Nesella returned the wet fields to their natural state. Palryma watched this incredible reformation from the other side of the rock fence. The wet fields began to burble and gurble as before. The dark, hollow pits returned to their echo-making sounds of the Simeeore boars. The warm and twirling breezes captured the yellow smoke from the noses of the boars and carried them past the purple onion trees on which they fed. The rare Shatoo birds once again darted back and forth in search of the green and pink argyle spotted snakes on which *they* fed. Three foot high willow 'o wisps surrounding the heaviest marshes sprouted back to life and whispered to only themselves in what was known to all who dared to enter the wet lands as the silly language.

"Mesella too ah keely ruinee," whispered one of the slim willows.

"Shemahba alloony srite," was the reply. Even the whispering willows knew what had just happened.

Nesella looked down upon what she had now restored to life and hoped that another chalice maker in the land would not be needed any time soon. "It is a difficult business indeed… drying up these wet fields," she mused.

"You did a perfect job, Nesella. More perfect than anyone in this old long line of chalice makers could have ever done. We are deeply in your debt. Without you we could not have had another chalice maker in the land. Thank you kindly for your work" said Batoowa.

"You are most welcome, your Grace," answered Nesella. "I am always pleased to oblige." "I think Palryma will make a wonderful chalice maker," she added.

"Yes he will. Yes!" chimed in Pormetah "Palryma will be the best ever. Yes he will!"

Batoowa closed the official bestowing of the special gift by saying "With the help of Sweet Lenora-ga he will succeed."

As for Palryma himself all he could add was, "Boy, I am glad I am not in there now," he said with a sigh of relief. "I have had enough of the wet fields for one day!"

"I wonder what ever shall I do now?" he thought almost absent-mindedly to himself.

"You will go along home to your parents now. That is what you will do," said Batoowa sternly. "They await you. The village of Goosra awaits you. There is still the matter of the wedding celebration tonight and your parents must be honored."

"Will they know already about…well…you know…. about all of what has just happened?"

"Yes. They will know. Everyone in the village knows and soon all in the land will know."

"Even Hurrah III?" asked Palryma hesitantly.

"Yes. Even Hurrah III." was Batoowa's quick reply.

Palryma was not sure what to make of that piece of news.

Not many in the land had ever seen Hurrah III and the stories about him were not good. In fact, they were often treacherous ones. He almost never left his castle atop the Dusky Hill and he was certainly not beloved by the people in the land. He was definitely not loved the way his father Hurrah II had been loved.

When Palryma was only 12 years old he tried to shoot down with arrows Hurrah III's talking bird, Settela. His aim back then was not as good as it was now and he only nicked the feared talking bird on the claw. But he remembered quite well the incident. Settella cawed and cawed and vowed to fly back to the castle to arrange for his revenge. "I will tell my master Hurrah about your arrows and you will soon be sorry the day you saw me in the air!" Later that evening, the dark-as-night flying Reelatta horses ominously swooped down from the castle and kicked the chimney off the roof of the cottage-where Palryma lived with his parents.

The next day some villagers helped repair it and afterwards lit a fire in the new chimney to honor Sweet Lenora-ga in the hope that no new attacks would occur. Palryma made a secret vow to himself before he closed his violet eyes to sleep that night that if he ever saw Settela again he would strike him through his heart with an arrow as sharp as the nasty yellow bird's tongue. "I will not stand for anyone attacking my parents," he vowed "Not now. Not ever!" But since that day, not once in the passing 11 years, had he ever seen Settela flying in the skies above the land again.

"How will I start this new life of a chalice maker?" asked Palryma.

"Go along your way now. Take your Shatoo birds' home for the wedding feast. Take joy in the gift we have now bestowed upon you," ordered Batoowa

Cooperative but unshaken by this momentous event, Palryma stooped to gather his firewood. "Will I just sit and wait to hear from you?"

Batoowa smiled graciously down upon Palryma. "No, my son. Simply go home to your parents. Go along and whistle your favorite walking songs as you return to Goosra as the land's new chalice maker. Do not worry, for your guides will be along by and by."

And so he did. Palryma slung the two huge Shatoo birds over his shoulder, carried the firewood under his arm and waltzed down the road towards Goosra whistling his favorite walking song. At peace and at ease, the 23-year-old hunter was heading towards the greatest adventure of his life.

Chapter Two

Palryma sauntered down the village road with seemingly not a care in the world. Had the big announcement not been made with a million musical notes, no one would have guessed that the cheery young man with sandy colored hair had just experienced what only three living persons in the land could even talk about. It was not Palryma's style, though, to become overly excited about anything. He had earned a reputation for being very level headed for such an adventure-some lad. His extraordinary hunting skills always seemed to have come easily to him — although he was known to practice them with a vengeance. It just seemed natural to him that he was very good at things. He was good at sharing his skills with other hunters, especially the young ones who looked up to him. But, as his walk brought him closer to the village, he asked himself out loud, "I wonder what is to become of me now — now that I am a chalice maker? I really have no idea how to proceed. I have never met Great Ben and I don't remember Billora. And I have no clue as to how I begin to make chalices. It really seems quite a mystery to me."

"I hear you, young Palryma," came the whisper so low that Palryma himself could not hear it. "I hear you and I see you." said the whisperer — this time a little louder. Just loudly enough so that the new chalice maker stopped in his tracks.

"Is someone there?" His quick eyes darted back and forth. He dropped the prized Shatoo birds to the ground along side the firewood and prepared to do battle. "Who whispers there from the forest?!" He spun around 360 degrees to scan the perimeter and saw nothing. "I'll ask politely only one more time. Is anyone there?"

Palryma felt a cool, direct breeze hit the middle of his back and he immediately turned around to take a stance against it.

"Oh my goodness no! Oh by rolly-toe!! I got you! I got you by rolly-toe!! I will kicky-kackle now forever! Shoonee-na Palryma — turn about! I am now where your front used to be!! Oh this is fun! I got you by rolly-toe!!!"

In an instant Palryma swirled around to confront the mystery voice. What he saw was the oddest-looking creature whose width was almost the same as its height. Its ears were very long in the lobe and square at the top. Its face bore the nose of a child and the beard of a grown man....and both were orange! There were three toes on each fat foot that wiggled when the smile underneath the orange beard widened. Palryma was dazed with puzzlement.

"You are not from the village, are you?"

This sent the creature up into the air with 20 spins and landed with a splat on the moss covered tree stump at the road's edge.

"Oh my goodness! The village? That makes me swanee-sump! Oh by rolly-toe! Do I look like a Goosra-ian? What a kicky-kackle you are young Palryma! This will be fun — you and me!"

"What do you mean "you and me"? What are you doing here if you are not from the village?"

"You'd better ask me what my name is. I don't want to be bally-wally with you!"

A mild frustration overcame Palryma as he peered down

at the creature through his squinted eyes. "I will tell you my name as I think that is the polite thing to do. If you then tell me yours, it is up to you. I am Palryma, son of Bestra and Merrilyee. I am from the village of Goosra. I was returning there to attend the wedding celebration of my parents before you interrupted my walk!"

This set the creature into another 20 spins in the air landing this time on his fat feet in the very same spot. His toes wiggled wildly as the edges of his smile nearly reached his long ear lobes.

"Sweet Lenora-ga! I already know who you are!"

"Then politeness dictates that you must now tell me who you are!" spoke Palryma

"Oh by crum-de-crum! You must learn to be more fun! If you smile I will show you my hands!"

"If you please....I would rather know your name."

The creature shook his long orange and black hair and scrunched up his baby nose.

"Oh all right. I won't be bally-wally with you."

The creature twirled in place eight times and stood on his tippy-toes before bowing at half waist before Palryma. "I am Dalo" he said with all the confidence of a forest schwimmy – bold, positive and ultimately very funny. "Dalo it is and Dalo you shall call me. Not Dallie, not Dalo-boy and certainly not Mr. Dalo. I am Dalo, young chalice maker. Dalo. And I am your guide."

"My what!?" Palryma was shocked. "You are my guide..... to what?"

"Now...do not raise a fuss or bally-wally it shall be! Did not His Grace, Batoowa inform you that your guides will be along by and by? I believe those were his exact words "by and by" were they not?"

"You know about the chalice maker rite?"

"Know about it! Oh crum-de-crum Palryma! I was there! I knew it was going to happen and Batoowa promised me that I would be one of your guides. I knew all about it!"

Palryma scratched his head and tried to recollect the initiation rite. "I...I...don't really recall seeing you there...I'm sorry. Truth is...I don't really recall too much about any of what happened after I saw Batoowa."

"Ah....as sure as my hair is black...no new chalice maker ever remembers too much about the initiation rite. It only comes back to them after a while. You'll remember. Give it time, by rolly-toe. Give it time!"

"Um....Dalo...not to be impolite but your hair is not black. It's a strange combination of orange and black."

Dalo swung his long hair in a circle around his pumpkin shaped head. "Oh...that! Well...that's a kind of a long story. It comes from hanging in the wet fields too long. But black is my natural color. I'm trying to get back to it and now that I am closer to the forest schwimmys, I am certain I'll soon be rid of all this orange."

"How long were you in the wet fields? I don't think I have ever seen you there and I have been hunting in there for ten years."

"Well" said Dalo sort of sheepishly, "I was in there for about 43,000 years...give or take a few. I'm not definitely certain."

"Did you fall victim to the Legend of the Wet Fields? Did the wetness start to seep into your boots until it was too late?"

"Weeeelll....you see young Palryma...there is a lot about the wet fields that you don't understand and an awful lot more that you have never seen."

"I know that I don't understand why I need a guide or why you were selected."

"Again," said Dalo "there is much you don't understand.

But I will tell you that I was not automatically selected ...I volunteered — begged was really more like it. 43,000 years was long enough to be stuck along the Big Marsh listening to those willow 'o wisps whisper to each other. That's where I learned the silly language. I heard it for so long that I can hardly stop talking it sometimes."

"Oh....is that what that is? I have heard of that Legend of the Silly Language but I have never heard it whispered from the willows."

"Hmmmm....well, blarty-too-ah — I have had to listen to it for 43,000 years. Enough is enough. I finally convinced Batoowa that I was most sorry for my crime and...."

Palryma stopped Dalo immediately. "What do you mean your crime?! There can be no criminals in the land."

"You're telling me!"

"What did you do, if it can even bear repeating? I have never known anyone who committed a crime."

"It was comparatively very small but also altogether very thoughtless. You see, I was a forest schwimmy when I went into the wet fields that fateful day."

Palryma could not believe his ears. Forest schwimmys were without question the most beautiful creatures in the forest.... some said they were the most beautiful creatures in all the land. They were not seen too often in or around Goosra but once in a while a few could be spotted. They were so beautiful they took your breath away. No one ever tries to capture them and most certainly they were not for eating.

"A schwimmy?!" gasped Palryma. "You were a forest schwimmy? Why did you go into the wet fields then? Everyone knows that forest schwimmys cannot make it out of there."

"Tell me something I don't already know," smiled Dalo. "I already know what you are thinking. You wonder how did something of such exotic beauty come into.....well...come into looking like me?"

Palryma was shamed by this thought. He knew better. "You'll have to admit, Dalo...your looks seem to have changed over the years."

"Oh, but mercy-mum-tum, I was something to behold," replied Dalo. "My problem was that I thought I was more beautiful than the gods. I actually thought my beauty was power and therefore I could do anything I pleased. So one day I very stupidly decided that I would rush into the wet fields and pick a Cannerallo Cupid flower for my love – just to impress her. I paid a dear, dear price for that foolishness."

Palryma put his hand over his mouth in horror. "Picking the Cannerallo Cupid flower is instant death!"

"Yes....yes...if you consider being stuck in the Big Marsh having to listen to the willow 'o wisps whisper their silly language for 43,000 years then yes....mine was an instant death."

"Whatever possessed you?"

"A beauty much greater than mine possessed me.....my love was all for another a forest schwimmy and she was reknown amongst us all for being the most beautiful of all time. I was insipidly in love with her but she barely noticed me. Imagine that! Hardly noticing someone as beautiful as me. I thought if I presented her with a Cannerallo Cupid flower she would accept my love."

"What happened?"

"As soon as I picked the flower the orange and black colors of it faded immediately and the flower disappeared from sight. I was thrust into the Big Marsh amongst the willow 'o wisps. I panicked and began to scream for help but I found I could shout no louder than a whisper. In an instant I became a whisperer amongst willow 'o wisp whisperers and no one could hear me. I was devastated and marked as well. I saw that the orange and black colors of the flower were now in my hair and my crime was thereby announced to anyone who could see me. Then the whispers grew so loud that I was certain I would lose my mind and I did something that sealed my fate for 43,000 years."

"What could you have possibly done that was worse than trying to pick a Cannerallo Cupid flower?

"I shouted a curse to Sweet Lenora-ga."

Palryma could not even speak. This simply could not be. No one in the land ever cursed Sweet Lenora-ga. As far as Palryma knew, it was unheard of.

"Why did the gods not kill you right then and there? How is it that you are even alive? And why is someone who cursed Sweet Lenora-ga my guide?!"

"Ah...crudey-ha me shat, Palryma. I have long since learned my lesson. I have begged and begged forgiveness and now it is mine. I have been released from the wet fields by Batoowa and he decided that I could be your guide. I will be a good guide. I know what I did was wrong and I know I will never be a forest schwimmy again. All I asked was that the insufferable tag of orange and black hair be removed from me. Batoowa said that as long as I was a good guide, my natural color would be returned."

"That's it? That is all that you asked for, Dalo — after 43,000 years? To have your hair turned black again?"

"Crickey-krackey — no Palryma....do you think I am cralee-hoo? I just told you I spent 43,000 years stuck in the Big Marsh. Even more than my black hair, I wanted my good heart back. That was the other thing. Even as an incredibly beautiful but foolishly-in-love forest schwimmy I had a very good and true heart...perhaps a bit misguided, I will now admit...but it was a good and true heart that my own parents gave me. I pleaded with Batoowa to release me and give me back my heart."

"Did he?"

"Yes. And as long as I remain a good guide to you, I will keep my good heart. So, you can rest assured that I will be a good guide! I will be sumpty-hara! The best!!

"Alright, I guess I will have to trust you. It is past mid-day though and I must get back to the village and help prepare these Shatoo birds for the wedding celebration of my parents."

"Well, by lumpty-nu, let's stop walking like marly mush bugs from the Big Marsh and get a move under our feet" exclaimed Dalo "We're headed to Goosra! Don't forget the fire-wood. That'll be very important tonight, by rolly-toe!"

Palryma picked up the firewood and slung the Shatoo birds over his shoulder again.

"By the way Pallie — when first we met you were whistling one of your favorite walking songs weren't you?"

"Pallie? Did you just call me Pallie! Who said you could do that?"

"I'm your guide....I can call you Pallie if I want to."

"But I cannot call you Dallie...is that correct?"

"You've got it now, by rolly-toe! You've got it! You can whistle away and I can thump along to any walking song you like with my big fat feet and my wiggly toes! And we'll just walk our way straight to Goosra."

"Goodness but you are not like anyone I have ever known. Are you sure you are suppose to be my guide?"

"No sumpty-swat about it Pallie! I am your guide. Oh, by rolly-toe this is going to be fun. You and me, Pallie! This will be great fun!"

And so their journey together began. Palryma just began to walk and whistle and Dalo just thumped along with his fat feet and wiggly toes.

"Whatever shall I tell my parents?" quietly wondered the new chalice maker "Whatever shall I say?"

Chapter Three

Palryma and Dalo made their way easily into Goosra and the closer they got to the village the more Palryma could see that villagers were gathered around in groups. Some stood in small crowds around the doors of their homes and some were gathered in front of the shops. There was no mistaking but they were all awaiting the arrival of the new chalice maker. Palryma's parents lived on the far side of the village so there was no way he could escape the adoring gapes from people he had known his whole life.

The first to acknowledge his presence was Bethnee, the wife of the village baker. The baker's shop was the first sight anyone could see on an approach to Goosra and both Bethnee and her husband considered it a gift from the heavens that they were able to build their shop where they did. It was perfectly placed for good business and anyone coming into or leaving Goosra was bound to stop at their bakery for some nourishment to take on their way or to take home after a long day.

As a child, Palryma would always get a special sweet coulda from Bethnee when he announced to her in the early mornings that he was going out to hunt for rare-bits and pig-nittys in the forest. Even in his early years, Palryma won the hearts of the villagers and Bethnee was keen to save a treat for little Palryma.

He always got a loaf of frosting-covered toody bread to take home after his day in the forest — whether he came home with nothing or, more likely as it was as he grew older, whether he came home with a side bag filled with pig-nittys for his favorite soup. Palryma was always rewarded for effort by Bethnee. Now that he was a chalice maker, though, Bethnee was unsure of what to give him. Her husband, Beeloma the Baker, told her to just let Palryma decide.

"Hello and heavens above Palryma!" shouted Bethnee as he drew closer to the bakery.

"Hello and heavens above to you, Bethnee! It's a very fine day is it not?"

"Well I guess for some of us it is a fine day and then for some others of us it's a remarkable day. How would you agree with me?!" she teased.

"I guess I will have to agree with you in every way possible. I guess maybe you have heard that I had a real turn of events in the wet fields."

"Oh Palryma," Bethnee gushed as he came to stand in front her now. "Beeloma and I are so happy and so dearly pleased for you and your parents. It is the gift of the gods to be chosen and only Sweet Lenora-ga could have seen this through. We bow to you". With that, Bethnee lifted her baker's apron and made a half waist bow to Palryma.

"Please...please Bethnee don't do that. It seems so strange and out of place. I am just Palryma who you have known since I was a child."

"True enough as the sun shines down on Goosra — but you are also now Palryma the Chalice Maker and everything will be different now."

"Well...I am still Palryma who loves the sweet couldas and the frosting on the toody-bread! Some things do not change!" He had a look on his face that he might bust apart if he did not have a sweet coulda.

Bethnee realized now that her husband was right. Palryma chose what the tasty gift from the bakery should be and it was what he had always loved — sweet couldas and toody bread! Beeloma came up from the cellar of the bakery where the fire ovens were and he poked his hairless head outside the door to see the new chalice maker.

"Hello and heavens above young chalice maker!" Beeloma was like a second father to Palryma and his shiny baldhead was always a sign to Palryma that he was nearing home.

"Hello and heavens above to you Beeloma. All the graces of Sweet Lenora-ga upon you. Thank you for your kind greeting."

"It is no more than a chalice maker deserves. You honor us by stopping by."

"I don't know how all this chalice making will go by and by but I know that I will never stop coming to the bakery — not as long as there are sweet couldas in the window!" Palryma reached out his arms to hug both Bethnee and Beeloma and they both could feel real warmth coming from his arms.

They knew legend had it that one of the signs of a real chalice maker was warm arms. When he released them from the hug Bethnee had tears in her eyes. She knew now that her adorable little Palryma was now gone to the past and the Palryma the Chalice Maker was standing before her.

"I'd like both of you to meet Dalo." Palryma said as he turned his palms upright in a greeting gesture. But in doing so he noticed the odd blank look on both faces of his baker friends. The long married couple looked at each other and shrugged.

"Ah...nutsy-rayo Pallie.....I forgot to tell you....all the excitement of the initiation and all. But the deal is that they can't see me unless I want them to!" said Dalo.

"But I want them to meet you Dalo! I insist!" To Bethnee and Beeloma, it appeared as though Palryma was talking to the sky.

They looked at each other very strangely and altogether not really sure what to do. "Maybe you would like to sit and have a nice cup of cardboard seed tea, dear. You know...just to rest yourself before you go home?" offered Bethnee very nicely.

"Do you see now how silly you are making me look?" huffed Palryma to Dalo.

"I can't let them see me Palryma. It's my hair. It's all orange and black. As soon as they see it they will know that I tried to steal a Cannerallo Cupid flower. I don't want them or anyone to know that. I just want to be a good guide!"

"Well, you leave me no choice then." replied Palryma tartly.

"My good friends," he said as he turned to Bethnee and Beeloma "you have been very kind to me all my life. I love you both nearly as much as I love my own parents. Your kindness had meant the world to me. You have been especially generous in your remarks on this special day for me. It is true that the gift of the chalice maker was bestowed upon me earlier today. I am certain of its importance but uncertain of its impact upon me. But what I am absolutely certain of is that the chalice makers of my line have granted me a guide.....someone whose purpose I am also uncertain of. However, he does exist and is standing next to me."

"Then let him show himself. He is welcome in our bakery." said Beeloma. "Is there some problem?"

Palryma told them the story of Dalo and the Cannerallo Cupid flower and how he was shy to present himself with his orange and black hair. Bethnee remarked that the gods must have forgiven him otherwise he could not have been set free to be Palryma's guide. Beeloma agreed.

"I repeat," said the baker, "let him show himself. If he is your guide he is welcome here and it seems to me and my wife that all is forgiven. We are not in the business of questioning the gods. We are only in the business of making the fine goods in our bakery!"

"And fine they are indeed" said Palryma with glee. "The best sweet couldas in the land!"

"And we are happy to let this guide named Dalo taste one if he will just show himself. I'm sure he will agree that we make, at the very least, the best baked goods in Goosra," tempted Bethnee.

They waited no longer. Dalo appeared next to Palryma in a whirl of blue and white twizzles. Palryma smiled, stretched out his hand and said in his most agreeable and polite manner. "Bethnee and Beeloma, I am pleased to introduce my appointed guide, Dalo. He is quite extraordinary looking would, you not agree? I believe he possesses the finest head of orange and black hair I have ever seen and his beard — such a beautiful and bright orange!"

"Hello and heavens above to you, Mr. Dalo," said Beeloma in a warm greeting. "My wife and I welcome you to our bakery."

"By rolly-toe!....I am Dalo...just Dalo....not Dallie or Dalo-boy and certainly not Mr. Dalo. I am Dalo, guide for the chalice maker. Only Dalo!"

"Then hello and heavens above to you, Dalo. Welcome," said Bethnee. "My husband and I agree with Palryma that you indeed have a fine head of hair.....a most interesting color combination!"

"Oh....that," murmured Dalo. "Well, I think it is crickey-krackey and in good time it will soon be all black. But if you like to look at it now I won't be bally-wally with you."

Bethnee and Beeloma had very little idea of what Dalo meant as they had never heard the silly language spoken before.

They shrugged their bakers' shoulders and rubbed their hands in front of their aprons. "Well.....um....won't you come inside and rest with a cup of cardboard seed tea....and perhaps one of our special sweet couldas. I am sure Palryma would like one!" offered Bethnee.

"I would love one" shouted Palryma, "but then we must get on home to my parents and help with the preparation for the wedding celebration."

"Its sounds goody-much to me," added Dalo. "I must warn you though that I have been resting for 43,000 years and therefore I am very well rested. But, I think I would like to taste these sweet couldas!" Dalo looked around the area suspiciously and asked Beeloma quietly, "You don't have any green and white argyle spotted snakes in your house do you? They are all over the wet lands. I can stomp on them with my fat feet if you require!"

Beeloma assured Dalo that the bakery was free of snakes or any other sort of animal for that matter. He did give his wife a very puzzled look, though, as they escorted this unlikely duo into their bakery home. Dalo had made quite an impression. Once settled around the star-shaped table in the kitchen, Bethnee served up piping hot cups of cardboard seed tea and a big stone grey platter of sweet couldas and toody bread with white frosting. Dalo told several hitherto strange and unknown tales of the wet fields and Bethnee recalled how Palryma used to stand at the road's edge of the wet fields and make silly faces at the Simeeore boars. "Oh he was very daring even as a 6 year-old," laughed Bethnee. "He would taunt the boars to see if he could make them jump the big rock fence."

"And then he would come back and tell us that he shot them through with his pretend arrows!" recalled Beeloma.

"You must understand, Dalo, that my father did not give me my first bow and arrow set until I was 10.....but I liked the idea of getting used to confronting the Simeeore boars" Palryma quipped in mock embarrassment.

"Mucky swat Pallie!! You were taunting the boars with no real arrows?? Loody-draw-me-do! I think you were doing it with no real brains either!" Do you know what happens if a live Simeeore boar ever jumps the rock fence at the wet fields?"

Beeloma and Bethnee huddled close. Palryma said, "Oh no, this doesn't sound good."

"Not good? By rolly-toe... you could have been done for! One of the many Legends of the Wet Fields is that if any of the Simeeore boars ever get free by jumping the rock fence it will automatically turn back into a Katoo-Sinta...the most fearsome monster in the land. You have to get them mighty angry for them to charge and jump the rock fence. It's almost impossible for them to do that because that's how Sweet Lenora-ga made them!"

"What are you talking about?" asked Palryma

"I told you Pallie that there was a lot you did not know about the wet fields. Part of my job as your guide is to inform you, as the new chalice maker in the land, about all the legends."

"So, inform me."

"Way, way back in the beginning of the land Sweet Lenora-ga was confronted by the most hideous of all creatures – the Katoo-Sinta......a monster of impossible description and loathing. She destroyed the monster in a legendary battle of will power which she won, of course. She banished the monster to the wet fields and changed it into the shape it is now.... so huge and fat and hairy with such tiny short legs...so short that they would most likely never be able to jump the big rock fence and therefore doomed to roam the wet fields forever. That is why the meat of the Simeeore boar tastes so sweet...it is a reminder to all who are fortunate enough to eat it of the victory of Sweet Lenora-ga over the Katoo-Sinta monster!"

Beeloma and Bethnee were stunned. They had never heard that legend before. "If we had known that Dalo, we would have told Bestra and Merrilyee and they would have stopped Palryma from his taunting."

"Ah...crickey-krackey baker couple! The gods were watching Pallie even back then. No harm would have come to him.... certainly none to the village of Goosra. No...they marked Pallie from a very early age indeed. They have been watching him for a long time!"

"Then it was always meant to be?" inquired Beeloma

"Always" replied Dalo "but there is much to teach him about being a chalice maker...and that will be my job!"

Palryma stood up from the table. "Perhaps, but not right now, my good guide. We should be off to my parents' home. There is much to do before the sun sets. Will we see you there tonight?" he asked his hosts.

"Wild Simeeore boars could not keep us away!" cheered Bethnee.

"Thank you both for your hospitality." said Palryma as he headed for the door.

"Dalo...would you like another sweet coulda to take with you?" asked Beeloma

Dalo thumped both of his fat feet on the floor and shook his hair "Musty mee-lo, no...not so much at this time. But I will be back again. Yes....you can bet, by rolly-toe, that I will be back here to this bakery again!"

Ending their visit with the village bakers, the new chalice maker and his guide walked towards the home of Bestra and Merrilyee greeting all the well wishers along the way.

Chapter Four

"There it is Dalo!" Palryma shouted "there...just near the Shimmery Pond and the row of Surrupta trees. Dalo followed Palryma's pointing finger and could see a lovely cottage a short distance away that was the home Palryma was obviously very proud to live in. "That's the home I was born in. The home of my parents Bestra and Merrilyee. Wait 'till you meet them. They are wonderful people....just wonderful."

Dalo noticed how Palryma beamed with joy when he spoke about his home and his parents. It was as though nothing else mattered. "I will have to tell him soon," muttered Dalo to himself, "for I am running out of time and road! I better get on with it or I'll find myself stuck back in the wet fields." He stopped in his tracks, thumped his fat right foot into the ground and said with a voice proclaiming a real announcement "Listen Pallie...there's something I have to say right here and now."

"What is it?" said Palryma as he began to wave in the distance hoping that one of his parents might see him approaching.

"I won't be going with you to your parents' home or attending the wedding celebration this evening. It's not my place to be there."

"Is this about your hair again Dalo?" questioned Palryma

with a bit of exasperation in his voice. "As you could tell earlier, it certainly made no difference to Bethnee and Beeloma. They could not have cared less! It will be the same with my parents once I tell them the story of it. They are very loving parents. All I have ever had to do was be truthful with them. They have never asked anything else of me. When they learn the truth about you and the Cannerallo Cupid flower they will be most forgiving. Trust me. I know them."

"No Pallie. This has nothing to do with my hair," answered Dalo most directly. "I must tell you that this is the last full night you will ever spend with your parents and, as such, there is no reason for me to be there as a guest or even as a distraction."

Palryma's face hardened. Dalo had just delivered a surprise blow to the very heart of Palryma's life – his home and his family. "What are you talking about? Now you are really talking the silly language. There is no way I will ever desert my parents. Nothing could make me do that!"

Dalo was patient with his explanation but firm nonetheless all throughout. He explained that all new chalice makers had to leave their homes. It was the way it was. It was legend. A new home in the forest was provided by all the former chalice makers in the line and Palryma was expected to live there to learn the ways of a chalice maker. "There's no arguing Pallie. It's just the way it has to be. I will come for you in the morning."

"No! A thousand million times no! I won't do it!" Who will take care of my parents? Who will bring them food? Who will watch over them and care for them? I do this! This is my job!"

Dalo was even more deliberate this time. "Do you want to wind up like Billora, son of Pantara the fishing net maker?"

He chose not to follow the wishes of the chalice makers in his line. He did not get properly trained in the way of the chalice maker and he thought he could misuse his powers! He wandered into Latima and has never been seen or heard from again! Now his sad father sits broken-hearted every day of his life hoping his son will return! Is that what you want to happen to your father?!!"

"Billora went looking for a cure for his father's blindness! What you say is not fair! He was trying to help his father!"

"Well...lumpty-shoo-ra! Pantara is still blind and no one knows where Billora is or if he is alive or dead....and believe me, if he wandered into Latima it would be a blessing if he were dead! So that whole adventure seems not to have worked out too well, wouldn't you agree?"

Palryma gasped audibly. He stepped away from Dalo and cautioned him "You can never, ever wish death on anyone in the land, Dalo. It is against nature. You cannot say that it would be better if someone were dead. It is against the spirit of Sweet Lenora-ga!! Take it back! Take it back immediately!"

"Oh...all right Pallie...I was trying to make a point."

"Take it back!" he commanded

"Well...all right, by rolly-toe...I take it back! But you have to listen to me. This does not mean you can never see your parents again. Surely, you can see them. But you can no longer live in their cottage. You are not a villager anymore, Pallie. You are a Chalice Maker. You have been chosen."

Dalo explained that the chalice makers in his line would now provide for Bestra and Merrilyee. They would have safety and supplies a plenty. They would want for nothing. Batoowa will see to it he told Palryma. Batoowa, Pormetah, Nesela and all the rest of the chalice makers in the line have already made plans to provide for Palryma's parents for the rest of their lives.

"But I have been hunting for them since I was a boy!"

"You are not a hunter anymore, Pallie. Perhaps in the excitement of the day you have not noticed yet, but your bow and arrows have been left back in the wet fields. And there they will remain forever. Didn't you realize that you walked back to the village with just the firewood and the two Shatoo birds. You no longer have need for any bows and arrows."

"None of this makes any sense. What is to become of me?"

"Don't be distressed Pallie. Have faith in me and the wise decision of Batoowa and his friends to select you as the new chalice maker. But you must follow me as your guide. I will always be with you."

"I won't know how to explain this to my parents. How will I tell them that I am leaving their home for good?"

"Didn't you just tell me that all they ever expected of you was to tell them the truth? I am certain that is what you said. And didn't you say that they were very loving parents? Then all you have to do is tell them the truth and they will understand."

"You have to help me Dalo. I cannot do this on my own," said a worried Palryma.

"My job is to guide you. It is your job to explain things to your parents. That is why I will not be at the wedding celebration tonight. You will be fine. Simply tell the truth."

"I fear I will ruin this special night for them. I fear I will cause them great unhappiness."

"By the faith that Batoowa has place in me as your guide I am really suppose to wait until I take you to your new forest home tomorrow to say this, but under the circumstances I think I will give you an important guide before you walk into your parents' home. Fear, Pallie, is the only thing I know of that gets you exactly what you want. Surely as a brave young hunter you must have sensed this. If you are afraid that you will not shoot down a Shatoo bird then you probably won't. If you are afraid that you cannot face down a Katoo-Sinta monster then you probably can't.

"If you are afraid that a pretty girl won't kiss you then you might sadly wind up trying to steal a Cannerallo Cupid flower. Do you see what I am saying? You have nothing to fear from your parents. They love you and you already know that very well. If you are happy they will be able to see it in your violet eyes. They have been looking deep into them since the moment you were born. Tell them what you have to do without any fear in your heart and they will understand. Make a wonderful wedding celebration for them this evening....one they will remember forever. Build a huge fire, tell tales, dance and sing. Whistle walking songs and thank Sweet Lenora-ga that you have been so blessed. What can be wrong with that?"

"Nothing, I suppose," replied Palryma quietly.

"Then go Pallie....go be with your parents. Show them how happy you are for them that this is the night of their wedding celebration. Tomorrow morning we will start our journey....that will be soon enough. I, myself, must leave now and your parents await. Fear nothing. Remember that Pallie. Fear nothing. Freh-nit high."

"What does that mean?" asked Palryma as he picked up the bundle of firewood.

"Good-gra-ha-ha, Pallie! I'm not suppose to tell you everything all at once...especially what the silly language means! But I will make an exception this time since it is our very first day of meeting. Dalo beckoned Palryma to bend down so he could whisper in his ear. "Freh-nit high" means "I'll see you soon." That's all — "I'll see you soon."

"Ok then Dalo. Freh-nit high."

Dalo disappeared into a cone-like whirl of red and green twizzles. Palryma, feeling a bit confused and left on his own, slung the Shatoo birds over his broad shoulders, picked up the bundle of firewood and headed for the easy comfort of his parents' home for the last time.

Sweet memories of his childhood came running across his mind as he drew nearer to the Shimmery Pond. He remembered his first walk along its shore with his father when he was four years old. He remembered the fun and games of Bibitelly and Flying Cape with his friends, Siglatee and Moralna. He remembered very clearly his first swim in the Shimmery Pond when he began to swim the stroke of Tarlatta the Champion without so much as one lesson.

Everyone in Goosra was most impressed with this feat, especially Tarlatta, but none more than Bestra who knew better than everyone except for Merrilyee that Palryma was a very special boy indeed. His parents delighted in watching their son grow each day. They loved seeing him romp outside with his friends, read his books silently by the fireside and watched him sleep peacefully through the night. He was a joy to them. "And now I must tell them good-bye."

Palryma wondered how he could manage to deliver this news, especially on this wedding celebration day. He looked at the row of massive Surrupta trees which dotted the perimeter of the Shimmery Pond and hoped he might gain some inspiration from their strength and beauty. They grew from seedlings and had been a tall, graceful presence at the Shimmery Pond since before the reign of Hurrah the Beloved. It was rumored that their roots traveled for miles and miles deep under the land and rose again well beyond the far side reaches of Latima.

No one had ever seen this as no one who had ever dared venture into the evil land of Latima was ever seen again.

Palryma's reminiscing came to an abrupt halt when his gaze focused upon his home. There he could see his parents waiting at the cottage door for their son, the Chalice Maker. They waived and smiled and they shouted with glee, "Hello and heavens above Palryma! Hello and heavens above to the new Chalice Maker!" Tears began to well in Palryma's violet eyes. "I don't think I want to do this," he whispered as he choked back the tears.

Bestra shouted out to his only son, "Will you not greet your parents on this special day!?" Palryma swiftly wiped the tears from his cheeks before his parents could see them. "Hello and heavens above Mother! Hello and heavens above my Father! Look what I have for your wedding feast!" He raised his strong arms high in the air. "Firewood and two big, beautiful Shatoo birds for the wedding table!" His gate increased as he rushed to embrace his beloved parents. "We require no more than your presence my son," said Merrilyee gently. "That is all we have ever wanted."

"But, my dear, the Shatoo birds will impress all our guests. We will have a feast tonight because of our son!" roared Bestra. Palryma set the fire wood by the door and dropped the Shatoo birds. "I do it all for you both. It is a day of celebration for only you." he said as he hugged both his parents at once. When he released them, they stepped back in a half bow. "We are reminded, Palryma, that a chalice maker has warm arms and you have now just demonstrated that to us. You are now a chalice maker and honor must be paid," said Merrilyee.

"It is true son" added Bestra "what your mother says is quite right. You are our son, but you also have had a special gift bestowed upon you today. We heard the announcement from the air above the land and we saw with our own eyes the musical notes as they floated to the ground."

Palryma begged his parents not to bow to him. He told them it broke the natural order of things for parents to bow. He wanted to be treated as they had always treated him.... with love, kindness and affection but never bowing. It made him wince when they did that. "It is I who must bow to you for all you have done for me."

"Not any more Palryma. Things will be different from now on. Our love for you remains as always, of course, but you must get used to the fact that you have been specially chosen and the natural order of things no longer applies to you."

"But father......"

"No more discussion of it," declared Bestra with a pretend huff and puff. "But, you can still help your mother prepare the Shatoo birds! Now that is something that cannot change!" Palryma began to laugh heartily for the first time that day. "Come inside Palryma," beckoned his mother, "and tell me about your day." She had repeated this welcoming invitation to her son for all his life. When she said it, he always knew he was home. "And I will begin to prepare the fire!" announced Bestra with a flourish. Palryma knew right then and there it would be a big fire and a fine feast. But he also knew he has one more piece of information to tell them.

"Later...I will tell them later," he said to himself. "After the wedding celebration is over."

Chapter Five

By the time the guests began to arrive at the home of Bestra and Merilyee that evening the gorgeous aroma of roasting Shatoo birds could be smelled wafting in the air as they approached the cottage. The crackling fire inside their home was small compared to the roaring one set by Bestra in the large space in between the back of the cottage and the edge of the Shimmery Pond. Small bowls of sindra eggs were placed carefully around the enormous wedding table that the villagers gathered around just outside the back door. Guests were encouraged to splatter them on toody bread or slices of foxandra.

To the left of the table was the roasting pit carefully attended by Palryma, who, with great care, evenly basted the birds with the special gillealla sauce made from the mixture of pig-nittys, crushed rare-bits and sweet forest flowers. It was a specialty of Merrilyee's and a favorite of Palryma's since he was a boy. Plates laden with red chelly fruits and toasted flat brown breekora leaves from the Surrupta trees were passed among all those celebrating the wedding feast.

The most special treat of all was the Kalento wine made from the bulbous Heardne flower which thrived only at the bottom of the Shimmery Pond. Each morning, for three weeks prior to the celebration, Palryma and Bestra had been diving into the pond at the exact moment of the sun's first hitting of the breekora leaves for that was the only time of the day when the Heardne flower was at its most bulbous and carried inside of it the juice for Kalento wine, named after the first villager of Goosra who discovered it. Palryma wanted his father to rest easy and let him do all the diving but Bestra insisted that he help because it was he who dove into the Shimmery Pond 24 years earlier to get the flowers for the wine at his own wedding ceremony.

"You may call me sentimental and silly, but I toasted the beauty of your mother with our first glass of Kalento wine on our wedding day," Bestra told Palryma. "I want to toast her beauty again in front of all our guests, so we have to have all four of our hands pull up the Heardne flowers from the bottom of the pond." So collect they did — father and son — until Bestra judged that they had enough flowers to make plenty of wine.

Bethnee and Beeloma were the first to arrive. In their wagon, they carried six trays of sweet couldas specially decorated with spots and friffels of raiseny-uhs. "Hello and heavens above Beeloma!" shouted Bestra from the side of the cottage. Beeloma jumped from the wagon and pointed with pride to the sweet couldas. "Hello and heavens above to you my friend. How would you agree that this is a fine and glorious night? And what is that I smell from the fire?"

"I would agree with you in every way I could that this is a very fine and glorious night," laughed Bestra "And that delicious smell comes from two Shatoo birds roasting — birds, I might add that were brought to this wedding feast by my son, the new Chalice Maker!"

"Ah, Sweet Lenora-ga, yes! How would you agree with me that this is a doubly special night."

"It is a night of great honor. Great honor indeed and we are pleased that you and Bethnee are here with us. And there is Kalento wine for everyone!"

"Kalento wine!" yelped Beeloma "then there will be singing and dancing 'till dawn!"

Bestra watched his baker friends bring their trays into the cottage and shouted another "Hello and heavens above," to Simmee-Sammy, the village historian as he walked down the road with the huge Book of Events under his arm. He recorded all the important events of Goosra in this book and tonight's celebration was to be no exception. "Hello and heavens above Bestra! I have already been very busy today!"

Bestra knew exactly what Simmee-Samme meant. The Mayor of Goosra followed the historian to the wedding celebration. Bestra was especially happy to see Palryma's best friends Siglatee and Moralna racing each other down the road. "They have not changed one bit since they were six years old," recollected Bestra silently, "always running about everywhere!"

"Bestra!! Here we are!" they waved jointly. "We whistled walking songs all the way over! Even as we were running!"

"Hello and heavens above boys! How is it that you are always running?"

They stopped short right in from of him. "You know, Bestra — we are men now, not boys. We are not six years old anymore!" smiled Moralna.

"No...of course not. I forget just like an old man!"

"I will guess that Palryma is at the roasting pit spreading gilleala sauce on the Shatoo birds," said Siglatee. "How would you agree with me Bestra?"

He clasped his hands together in laughter. "I will have to agree with you all the way Siglatee, as much as you will have to agree with me that by the end of this wedding celebration your hands will be sticky as schmoona paste from eating too many sweet couldas!"

They darted away from Bestra and lit out for the roasting pit at the back of the cottage. "I will have to agree with you later Bestra," yelled Siglatee as he turned, "but now we must find our best friend and ask him about the Rite of the Chalice Maker!"

The line of villagers was growing and Bestra beckoned all of them to walk right in and make themselves happy and hearty. It seemed like the whole village was there to wish Merrilyee and Bestra another 24 years of sunshine and love and then another 24 years after that. Mikraught, the village tale-teller was only too ready to remind the guests that Bestra was the finest cobber in all the land when he married Merrilyee.

Cobbing paid little and Bestra decided to learn the magic of smoothing stones in order to place toody bread and lumb-wishes cake on the eating table. "It was none other than Loora, helper of all things to Hurrah II who taught Bestra to be a cobber," recalled Mikraught. "Loora was gifted in all things, but especially in cobbing. He taught Bestra well." Everyone nodded in agreement.

Swee-Hara, the forest cleaner gave all at the table an idea. "Let us ask Bestra to favor us with a cobbing! It is a great night and maybe before the Kalento wine is served, Bestra will cobb us one for the memory of old times in Goosra." Merrilyee agreed that Bestra was the finest cobber in the land and Palryma knew first-hand that since his early boyhood his father's cobs comforted him, made him happy and filled his young hunter's heart with glee. "Yes, Father..maybe just one cobbing before we start the feast!"

"Oh I really wanted to toast my beautiful wife but I will

do that after the Kalento wine. So now you will all have to listen to me speak twice tonight! How will you agree with me on that?!" They all shouted in unison, "In every way possible!"

"This is the last cobbing I did before I learned the magic of smoothing stones. It has a special place in my heart for it reminds me of diving from the very top of the highest Surrupta tree to the bottom of the Shimmery Pond to get Heardne flowers for my young and beautiful bride, Merrilyee." Bestra took a long breath and began:

> Five wallers, ten wallers — ready, forward I spring
> Weightless, lovely — I grab the ring
> Reach for sunbeams, I make it clear
> Why Sweet Lenora-ga chooses me as her bombardier
> A fireball of somersaults ignites my show of shows
> Twisting and diving I am hungry for
> The wetness just below
> In like a knife, curtain down
> All wondering just when
> I will surface with not one Heardne flower
> But ten!!

Bestra bowed to his guests and kissed his wife on the cheek. "I think it is a good thing that I learned the magic of smoothing stones!" he joked. But all the guests clapped loudly and agreed that it was a very good cobbing, indeed. The laughter and merriment was at high pitch and the Shatoo birds were almost fully cooked. Palryma had the cutting knife ready to slice the meat as it turned on the roasting pit. He turned his back to the crowd gathered at his parents' home and barely whispered to himself "I am going to miss all this. I don't understand why I have to go away."

The huge fire made the dancing easy to see from Hurrah III's perch high atop his castle tower and the singing rang a foul and flat noise in his ears. "Why is there merriment in Goosra tonight?" he demanded of his talking bird, Settela. "It is music, my Lord," was the reply. Hurrah covered his ears and shouted back, "I don't like it!!! Make it stop. Fly down there and make it stop!" The bird became quite nervous at this command because there was no telling what might happen to him if he confronted the whole village with a command from Hurrah III. "But, my Lord, surely it will stop on its own... perhaps when they have all had too much Kalenta wine."

Hurrah was unrelenting. "I want it stopped now," he demanded. "Why are they making music at all?" Settela did not know how to phrase his response without mentioning the Rite of the Chalice Maker. He decided to tell a half-truth only. "It is the wedding celebration feast of Bestra and Merrilyee, my Lord....I believe you know them. Do you remember when you sent the dark-as-night flying Reelatta horses down there to kick the chimney off their cottage after that nasty Palryma tried to kill me and shed a disgrace upon this castle?"

"Yes, yes...I recall that incident well," he replied with his unmistakable snarl. "And now that loathsome hunter has been chosen to be the new chalice maker. Damn him any-way...he has always been protected and I do not know why. What magic does he possess?"

"Surely no magic greater than what your father Hurrah II gave to you and exists right here in this Castle, my Lord! There is none greater in the land."

Hurrah III threw his empty bowl of graces at Settela and knocked him off his perch. "Do not speak of my father you ignorant bird! I told you never, ever to speak of my father!"

The sharp-tongued bird barely recovered from the blow when Hurrah III issued his dictate. "Fly down to the wet fields immediately and retrieve for me the bow and arrows of Palryma." Settela's feathers turned white in an instant. "But the wet fields cannot be entered at night, my Lord. Danger and monsters abound!"

"Do as I say!!" The force of Hurrah's fearsome command knocked Settela off his perch once again. "Bring them to me. I will see what magic they possess. Tomorrow morning when he finally leaves the home of his parents, we'll see just how far he gets into the forest without them." Settela was cowering so in the corner that he could hardly take flight. Hurrah reached down and scooped the frightened bird off the floor and flung him with a dangerous force out the castle window. "Go!!!" he yelled.

So, Settela, the talking bird of the Castle of Hurrah III made a shaky but swift flight down from the Dusky Hill past the merriment of the wedding celebration directly towards the wet fields worried and wondering all the time if he would ever make it back from there alive.

Meanwhile the celebration for Bestra and Merrilyee continued with dancing and singing the likes of which had not been seen in Goosra since Palryma brought home the Simeeore boar five years ago. Bestra gave the best toast of the night when he quieted the crowd to tell them the story of how he met his beautiful wife 24 years earlier. "I was a wandering cobber....nothing more and thought I would happily remain so all of my days. But, the very day I wandered into Goosra from my home I saw this vision of beauty leaving the bakery carrying a basket of some freshly baked goods. I was paralyzed with her beauty! Without thinking, I immediately walked right up to her and asked her if she would like a free cobbing!" Merrilyee laughed at the memory of it all. "I was shocked that a man would approach me in such a way - especially one who was not from the village."

"It was horrible what she did to me next!" feigned Bestra.

"It was only what you deserved. I had to push you away with one of my sweet couldas!"

"A waste of one of my sweet couldas," cried Beeloma from his seat at the table. "I was watching the entire scene from my bakery window!"

No man in the land would ever dream of approaching a strange woman without first being introduced by another. It was considered to be very impolite. "But I had no one to make an introduction and I feared this wonderful woman would just waltz down the road and away from me forever," said Bestra quite fondly.

"It was exactly what I was trying to do!" teased Merrilyee. The guests roared with approval at her gentle humor. Bestra told all his guests that the next thing he did was dash into the bakery and buy one crusty frablip, the least expensive item in the baker for it was all he could afford. As he gave Beeloma the half-qualta rye and the promise of a free cobbing in exchange for the frablip he made the customary gripping of hands with the presentation of his name. "I am Bestra, a cobber from the village of Rahno and I beg of you sir, if you know that pretty young woman who walks away from your bakery, please introduce me as I fear my heart will sink into my boots and I will never cob again if I do not meet her."

"I could see right then and there that they were meant to meet and I agreed with no delay," interjected Beeloma. "It was my best introduction ever! How would you all agree with me on that?!"

"In every way possible!," was the unanimous response for all the villagers for they knew the marriage of Beeloma and Merrilyee was blessed with more sunshine and love than they could have possibly hoped for when they first met outside the bakery.

"She is every sweet forest flower I have ever seen and my bowl of graces is filled by nothing more than the very sight of her. My dear friends, I propose to you that my love for Merrilyee, mother of our son Palryma, the new chalice maker, will grow deeper than the roots of the Surrupta trees and will emblazed my heart with a glow brighter than any ever seen from the Shimmery Pond. She is my breath and I toast her on this our wedding celebration night."

The roar and shouts from Bestra's toast echoed all the way up to the Dusky Hill and inside the walls of the castle, Hurrah III made a secret vow to himself. "That ridiculous toast will sink deep into the Big Marsh in the wet fields after I get the new chalice maker's bow and arrows in my hands. Gentle Merrilyee will regret the very day of Beeloma's intro-duction. I will see to that. There will be no more protection for those three!!"

In Goosra the sky was turning purple, a sure sign that the sun would soon hit the leaves of the Surrupta trees waking the Winnaka birds to flight. Many of the wedding celebra-tion guests had long since departed wishing much sunshine and love to Bestra and Merrilyee as they walked down the road. Palryma asked Siglatee and Moralna to stay behind as he wanted to ask them something before they left.

The three boyhood friends gathered near the fading embers of the roasting pit and shared the last bits of the Shatoo birds that were left on the big serving plates. "I should have gone hunting with you in the wet fields Palryma. Then we would both have been chosen as Chalice Makers," mused Moralna. "It was only my luck to go looking for wallop-rums in the forest today to bring to the wedding celebration!"

"I don't think that is how it works, Moralna. I think I was meant to be there alone. At least from what I remember, it seemed that they had decided upon me for some time."

"I still don't know why you cannot remember everything that happened to you, Palryma," wondered Siglatee. "How is it that such a momentous occasion leaves so many holes in your brain?"

"I cannot answer all of these questions as I still have too many of my own. I agree with you that this is indeed a curious day but I cannot think of that right now."

Palryma huddled close with his two best friends and made his last request. "I must ask you both to come visit with my parents each Baking Day. If they have any needs, you must promise me that you will take care to oblige them."

"But where will you be?" asked Moralna. Palryma explained that he must leave home this very morning with his guide and learn the ways of the Chalice Maker. "I do not understand why I have to leave my home, but I am told that I must not question it. I can no longer live here and I am also told, if you can believe this at all, that I will no longer have any need for my bow and arrows." His friends were dumfounded. "No need to hunt!?" they exclaimed. "What will you do? How will you survive?"

"I don't know. I simply must have faith that this is what

I have been chosen to do and I must do it. But I am worried for my father and mother. My guide tells me that my parents will be well provided for but I want to make certain that they do not become lonely. You must promise me that you will call upon them for as long as I am gone."

"And how long will that be?" asked Siglatee. Palryma told the truth, as always. "I cannot say for certain for I think others will judge when I have learned the ways." Moralna stroked his long hair and said "We are your best friends Palryma and it will be an honor for us to call upon your parents each and every Baking Day until you return! But whatever happens to you in the forest, you must never forget that I, Moralna and Siglatee right here next to me are your best friends. We will always be that. I do not know who this guide of yours is, but if ever he requires help from your two best friends then he must show himself and we will run to you."

"And as you know full well Palryma, we are very, very fast runners!" added Siglatee. Palryma chuckled at this reminder and said "His name is Dalo and believe me if he ever does present himself to you, it will be impossible to forget!"

"Then it is set." declared Moralna "We must now wish your parents sunshine and love and then run home." Palryma hugged his friends, bade them farewell and he watched them poke their heads inside the cottage window to say goodbye to Bestra and Merrilyee. As he watched them run up the road he spoke softly "Freh-nit high my best friends. With the help of Sweet Lenora-ga, Freh-nit high."

The wedding celebration night was now officially over and the new chalice maker turned towards the cottage door to step inside and say good-bye to his parents.

Chapter Six

The explanation was unnecessary and the calmness of his parents took Palryma by surprise. "We knew already. Pantara told us last night at the wedding celebration. He asked us when you were going away," reported Merrilyee. "Ah, yes...the poor old fishing net maker is still broken-hearted these many, many years later over the disappearance of his son, Billora. You will not disappear will you Palryma? You will follow the instructions of your guide, won't you?" said Bestra "For it will surely crush us indeed, your Mother and I, if we had to suffer day in and day out the way Pantara does."

Palryma was at a loss for words. He could only see how serene his parents looked at this moment. He was sorry that he had waited so long to tell them. He did not want the news to come from Pantara. He promised himself at that very moment to return to his home as soon as his learning was done. "I will not disappear Father. I will never just go away and not come back. I give you my word on this." Merrilyee looked both pleased and relieved to hear this. "You have always been such a good son." she said. "Yes, a fine son indeed but as we all three know, a bit on the headstrong side of things. How would you agree with me on this?" Palryma was a shade embarrassed but said "Yes, you are correct Father. I will have to agree with you in every way possible. I was somewhat headstrong as a boy."

"You still are." said his Mother as she brushed the sandy hair away from his violet eyes.

"But I promise to you Mother that I will follow the instruction of my guide. I will learn the ways of a chalice maker and then I will come home to Goosra."

"We will be waiting for you, my son. We will always be here waiting for you." said Bestra with a choke in his voice. He tried to clear it away by saying "Now where is that guide of yours?" I want to meet him. What did you say his name was? Does he know that it is considered very impolite not to be on time?"

"His name is Dalo, Father. I think I should go outside the cottage and see if he is approaching. He said I should be ready to go in the morning."

"Well...it is certainly morning now. I can see the Winnaka birds flying in the air above the land and the Surrupta trees have turned themselves around to face the sun. Let this guide show himself!"

"When he does Father, don't be alarmed by his looks which are very interesting, of course, but may shock you at first."

"Sweet Lenora-ga, what does this guide look like?!" said Bestra.

With no warning, a tan, blue and butter-colored spin of twizzles appeared instantly before Palryma and his parents. The spinning twizzle stopped so abruptly that when he fell out of it, Dalo lost his balance and did three rolls on his side. He jumped right up and shouted with outstretched arms "Well..by rolly-toe! I look just like this!!" Bestra and Merrilyee looked at each other in pure wonder and amazement. Palryma saw the strange look on their faces and moved quickly with an introduction.

"Mother....Father....I would like you to meet my guide, Dalo. Dosen't he have a fine look about him?" Bestra and Merrilyee were speechless. "Dalo is going to teach me the ways of a chalice maker. How would you agree with me that he is a fine choice?" Between them there was more silence than inside of a soft cloud until Merrilyee spoke. "My husband and I welcome you to our cottage, Mr. Dalo. We are happy for this introduction." Bestra tried to smile but his lips had dried up and would not move.

"Rick-tee-norah-shaw!! This is true crickey-krackey! So you are Pallie's parents! Then you must know that I am Dalo.....Dalo it is and Dalo you shall call me! Not Dallie, not Dalo-boy and certainly not Mr. Dalo. I am Dalo and I am Pallie's guide!" At the end of his introduction, Dalo flipped himself twelve times in the air and landed flat on his back. "Oh, by crum-de-crum, I will have to work on that flip won't I, Pallie?!"

Finally, Bestra's lips were able to part and he looked at his son "Pallie?" He shook his head. "What kind of word is that? What does that mean?"

Palryma tried to answer quickly "Oh...it's really nothing Father....I think it is just a shortened version of my name."

"A shortened version? I don't understand. At birth, your mother and I gave you the name of Palryma." He looked at his wife "Merrilyee do you understand what this "Pallie" word is? Is it the language of some other land?" At this point she could only shrug her shoulders.

"Oh this is fun! What a crickey-krackey cottage this is! You can figure it out of course! Dalo cried with laughter as he lifted his foot "Look how I can whack my big fat feet and wiggle my toes!" I can tell you about my orange and black hair but not right now. We have to go!" He thumped one fat foot in front of the other and turned around "Come now Pallie. We must be off to the forest. Its time for you to learn the ways of a chalice maker."

Palryma found time to quickly hug his parents one more time. They handed him a small cloth bag. "It's just something to help you along your way, son" said Merrilyee. "Yes, and something also in there to remind you of your mother and me." added Bestra.

Palryma felt rushed and confused but he held his parents close one more time. "Thank you both for everything you have done for me. Thank you for being such wonderful parents. I promise that I will think of you every day."

Bestra could not help himself but ask one more question. "Palryma, are you certain that this Dalo fellow was selected be your guide?"

"Yes, Father...he is my guide. But actually, he told me that he volunteered for the job."

Dalo yelled back to Palryma "We must move along Pallie... we have a long way to go."

Bestra and Merrilyee watched their son run to catch up with the strange looking guide. "Is this not an unusual way for us to begin our 25th year together, Merrilyee? How would you agree with me on that?" His beautiful wife nodded "In everyway possible, Bestra. In every way possible." They turned and walked back into their cottage hoping that with the help of Sweet Lenora-ga their son Palryma would succeed.

Back in the Castle of Hurrah III the lonesome ruler waited impatiently for Settela to return from the wet fields. "I want this chalice maker's adventure ended before it begins its first steps into the forest. I swear that as long as I wander in this cursed castle there will be no more of them in the land as long as I am alive." he groused as he looked for any sign of Settela in the morning sky. "Where is that foolish bird?" he demanded to no one. He walked circles around his potion cabinet and cursed the day he ever gave the yellow bird a voice. The faint sound of flapping wings distracted Hurrah III from his regrets and reminiscences. With barely any strength left, Settela landed with great difficulty on the castle window's stone ledge. He was hardly able to lift his head. His master strode directly over and gazed meanly at the gasping bird. Showing no concern for Settela's exhausted condition he barked in a voice seething with anger "What took you so long? I see no bow and arrows in your claws! Why is that, Settela? Have you failed your master!?"

In addition to being exhausted, Settela was now dangerously frightened. He was all too familiar with the tone of Hurrah III's voice and knew all too well what evil deeds of which he was capable. "I....I....I beg of you my Lord....the wet fields would not yield." He lay prostrate on the ledge. "It was impossible. The bow and arrows were sunk into the Big Marsh....I...I..was not able....could not retrieve them. I was charged by the Simeeore boars and was nearly swallowed by the Galoota Eaters! Sir...I beg your royal mercy. It was nighttime and all the bestial forces were alive in the wet fields. I was outnumbered and overcome by the powerful friends watching over this new chalice maker. Please do not kill me, my Lord......I beg of you!"

Hurrah's beady eyes narrowed into pin-size and his brow curled into menacing furrows. He spoke not a word as he raised his right hand. The echoing force of his scream against the barren castle walls almost caused Settela not to see where his hand was headed. Hurrah took the quivering bird by the left claw and hurled him from the stone ledge to the cold castle floor ripping his claw off in the process. "I gave you a direct order!!! It was a command from your Lord and Master!! It was I, Hurrah III, who sent you on this mission and you DARE return to me with nothing! NOTHING?!! By this time Settela was nearly unconscious and in pain too great for a bird to bear. "You will leave my sight and sound and you will never return to this castle again. You will make your sorry way out there" as he pointed to the land at the edge of the Dusky Hill "see then how you can survive without me you disgraceful fowl. Survive on your own!! GO!!" With that pronouncement, Hurrah grabbed the nearly dead bird and hurled him out the window with the force of a thousand goulish winds. Settela tried with whatever diluted strength he had left in him to flap his tortured wings but to no avail. When the winds and the force of the throw stopped carrying him through the air, he landed with a thud deep into the forest, far from the palace, hidden amongst a large patch of the forgetful flowers and left for dead.

Palryma and Dalo walked down an unmarked path through the forest saying nothing for the longest time. Elongated rays of the sun beckoned both of them towards a place unknown. Even the thumping of Dalo's fat feet was muffled by all the thoughts twirling around inside Palryma's head. The only real noise was made by Palryma's whistling of his favorite walking songs. He finally broke the silence by saying "I feel different without my bow and arrows with me." Dalo did not reply....merely kept looking for a sign — something to let him know that they were approaching the place to begin showing

Palryma the ways of a chalice maker. "Did you hear me, Dalo? I said I feel..."

"Yes, Pallie. I heard you very clearly with my big long ears. You said you feel different without your bow and arrows. Let me tell you that it's not the last time you will feel different. It is a good sign. Soon enough...in time....you will BE different. Have patience."

Palryma simply looked at his guide. "I wonder too much about the things you say, Dalo. I don't understand half of them. Did it ever occur to you that maybe I don't want to BE different."?

Dalo flipped himself forward in three somersaults and faced Palryma while walking backwards. "You already ARE different! You have been chosen. Be grummy-soo....I think you know that already! The change has started...its just not complete yet." Palryma shook his head in exasperation and stuffed his hands into his pockets. He looked glum. He wanted to speak but was unsure of what to say. He did not want to be impolite. But finally he took his hands out of his pockets and thrust them towards Dalo. "Don't you see? Look at my hands. I am used to having the bow and arrows in them. I am used to hunting! What do I do with them now?"

"No more hunting for you Pallie. That is for certain. Your hands will forever more be used for chalice making. That's it! No bally-wally about it."

This brief exchange only resulted in more silence as the chalice maker and his guide continued their walk deep into the forest. When words were finally spoken, it was Dalo who broke the silence this time. "Say, Pallie! That was a goody-much song you were whistling a while back there. What is the name of it, if I may ask?"

"I don't remember." Palryma said with an approaching

petulance in his voice.

"Of course you do Pallie! By rolly-toe, I'll bet you even invented the song all by yourself. That's how clever you are! Come now – tell your beautiful guide the name of that nice whistling tune."

"They are called walking songs, if I may tell you." Palryma responded coldly "And I don't want to talk to you."

"By crum-de-crum Pallie, you will send me into a twizzle of twizzles!! With that, Dalo was encased in bright yellow and violet twizzels. They spun and spun and then disappeared almost as quickly as they showed up. Dalo was left in the middle of the road with an odd, quizzical look upon his face. Palryma crouched down to see if he was alright. Dalo looked at him strangely and said "Pallie give me your hands. Put them in mine." Palryma obliged and began to speak.

"No...no..Pallie. This is not your time to speak. It is your time to listen." He took a long deep breath and grasped Palryma's hands tightly. "I am your guide Pallie, I do not mean to hurt you or embarrass you by the way I look or make you bally-wally with me. But I have been given this job to do and I could surely use some help from you in getting it done, by rolly-toe. I have never been a guide before and you have never been a chalice maker before...so we are in this together. When you tell me that you don't want to talk to me, I fear that I am doing a bad job as your guide. If I do a bad job as your guide, Batoowa will send me back to the wet fields and I will have to listen to those shaggootry-blaw willow 'o wisps for another 43,000 years and then I'll never get my beautiful black hair back – ever! So what do you say, Pallie. Let's try to make this adventure fun. You and me."

"I am very sorry I was impolite, Dalo. I was letting frustration and fear of the unknown overcome me. I am very sorry

I caused you to get caught up in a twizzle. I will try to have fun from now on. Really I will."

"Sir-righty-roo!!" shouted Dalo "Let's get started again! Now tell me the name of that nice walking song."

Palryma was a bit embarrassed but he told Dalo anyway. "Oh...that one...well...it's a song I made up when I was 21 years old. I was returning to Goosra after a good day of hunting in the wet fields and I got to thinking about when I might ever....or would ever... fall in love and I started to whistle this song as I was walking back home. I call it "One Love for Me". I know that it may sound a bit silly but...."

Dalo interrupted Palryma instantly. "Silly!? Crum-sham and tooly nika. I think it is very beautiful! I think you have music in your heart Pallie. Yes, by rolly-toe, I surely do! Why it's a very catchy tune indeed. That's why I wanted to know the name of it. I think I can thump this tune out with my big fat feet as we walk along!! Let's try it Pallie!"

So the chalice maker and his guide continued to make their way down the road whistling and thumping but mostly laughing with each other.

"Dalo" asked Palryma in between verses "do you think I will ever meet someone? I mean, not to be impolite, but are chalice makers allowed to marry?" He paused for a moment and looked around. "I'd like to meet someone much like the one I had in mind when I first whistled "One Love for Me". He paused again "I hope she is beautiful."

"I have faith that you will, of course, meet someone one day Pallie. It would be a fine wedding day in Goosra, I am sure of that by rolly-toe! We will keep a keen eye out for her, you and me. We may just find her in the forest one day. You never know! But, as your guide I must tell you that its better that you hope you fall in love with her first and that she also falls in love with you. Then you will see each other's real beauty. I don't want to find that you have strayed off to steal any Cannerallo Cupid flowers!" Palryma roared with laughter at the very notion of repeating the former forest schwimmy's horrible mistake. "No, Dalo...have no fear...I will never do that for any woman - no matter how beautiful I think she is!"

"Good. Glad to hear that at least!"

"Dalo" said Palryma "if I may be permitted, I'd like to ask you another question."

"Anything you want, Pallie. Anything you want!"

"Not to be rude or anything...but do you have any idea at all where we are headed?"

Dalo continued to walk for a moment and finally said. "Not a clue."

"Hmmmm....I didn't think so. I guess that's all right, though."

"Just keep whistling the beautiful walking songs Pallie and I will keep thumping along. We'll get there by and by. You and me."

And so they did.....they kept whistling and thumping their way through the forest.

Chapter Seven

It was not long before the sky began to turn its soft color of pink and orange indicating with no question that the day was ending and night was soon to rule the land. Dalo and Palryma had walked far, far into the forest – way beyond Goosra. Palryma saw for the first time the Loo-Hoo-Hoo trees that he had only heard about as a boy from Mikraught, the village tale-teller. He never dreamed he would be standing next to one. They grew from small yellow bushes into the tallest trees in the forest with trunks so wide around that one had to rest before making the full circle and they had branches no longer than an arrow that protruded all they way to the top of the tree – so high that the branches on top looked like little dressing pins from the ground. Each branch was covered in hundreds of tiny windalee flowers of bright and shiny blue. "If you ever see a Loo-Hoo-Hoo tree" Mikraught told Palryma when he was nine years old "you must be sure to make a wish upon it as you place your hand upon its massive trunk. It will surely come true as it is a legend of Sweet Lenora-ga." Wishes were rarities in the land and Palryma never forgot Mikraught's advice. He placed his hand on the flower covered tree trunk and said "I wish to meet the one I love."

Dalo watched Palryma from the ridge over looking the sloping gulley. "I saw you, Pallie!" he shouted down to him "what did you wish for, eh? A new guide perhaps?"

"I want no other guide but you Dalo...how would you agree with me on this!?"

"What then!!? Did you wish to learn the ways of a chalice maker?"

"I wished for something special!" was Palryma's reply preferring to keep his wish to himself.

"Well, if you wished to see the very place where you will learn the ways of a chalice maker, your wish has already come true for we are here Pallie! We are finally here! Come to the ridge and see!"

Happy and relieved to have the forest walk finally at an end, Palryma dashed up to the top of the ridge and stood next to his guide. In the gully below him, he saw a clear brook running in swirls around a large cave that was completely covered in the unforgettable violet and yellow colors of the forgetful flowers. Gold brook fish hopped up from the water to dance on their tail fins before jumping up just high enough to dive back into the brook. A short chimney made of magic smoothing stones billowed into the air the pure absolute white smoke ascending from the burning branches of the mistra bush in the cave's hearth. Kura birds sat above the entrance to the cave and chirped the harmonious overture that happily welcomed the two new visitors. "Oh, by rolly-toe, Pallie — it looks like we have been well provided for here. We have come to a good and warm place to learn. Batoowa was right. He said I would know the place to teach you the ways of a chalice maker as soon as I saw it!" He was lit up with glee as he looked at Palryma "We are home, Pallie! We are finally home!"

Dalo began to run down the steep decline towards the cave and tumbled in successive somersaults over his fat feet and wiggly toes. When he stopped tumbling he landed no more than a few feet from the cave's entrance. He shook his head in an attempt to clear it from the tumble. "When I was a forest schwimmy, I would have floated easily down to the cave" he laughed "ah...but those days are long gone and so it is. I am a guide now and have successfully brought this new chalice maker to his appointed home." He looked around the area and decided that, as he saw from the ridge, this was a fine place indeed. "Come on down Pallie" he beckoned "all is clear! Watch how you tumble, though!" Palryma had no trouble descending the ridge. He was sure-footed and nimble and nearly hopped all the way down. When he reached the cave, he made motions with his hands to dust Dalo off. "That was quite a tumble, Dalo" he teased "are you very sure you are recovered?"

"Oh that....it was my fat feet...nothing more. I, too, really am quite nimble!"

"Of course you are." said Palryma "I could easily see that myself! I hope you will stick to teaching me the ways of a chalice maker and not try to teach me how to become more nimble!"

"Harruumph" replied his guide. "I will pray to Sweet Lenora-ga that your humor improves along with your chalice making!" The easy banter between the guide and his chalice maker faded as they both walked hand in hand towards the entrance to the cave. "How do we enter?" asked Palryma. Dalo looked sharply for some sign and decided that it must lie beneath the sheath of forgetful flowers that encased the cave's entrance. "Look over there, Pallie...in the middle of the drop below the Kura birds. Run your arm under the flowers...see if you can find a soft spot in the rising. Palryma followed the instructions and used both hands and arms to look for a way in. "Anything?" asked Dalo. Palryma shook his head. Dalo stepped closer and motioned for Palryma to inspect the area a little lower to the ground. Complying with his guide's wishes, he pushed and pulled at the cascading blanket of flowers while trying very hard not to crush them.

"Maybe there is a secret word to open the cave?" suggested Palryma "maybe it is something from the silly language...... how would you agree with me on that?"

"I would not agree with you at all" replied Dalo. "Try over there...on the opposite side."

As soon as Palryma did that, a loud grinding noise began that startled both of them so much so that it caused them to jump back in shock. "Something is happening here, Dalo.... what is it!?" Palryma said as he covered his ears to muffle the loud grinding sound.

"You've done it, Pallie!! I have never heard such a racket before but I think that this is the sound of the cave door opening. We are in, by rolly-toe. We are in!"

They watched as the forgetful flowers separated themselves. The part of them that covered the cave door slowly opened inwards until it stopped leaving only a gaping entranceway for the two travelers to walk through. "You first, Pallie" said Dalo quietly "after all, you are the chalice maker!"

"And you are the guide...so it is who you must go first and guide me in!"

Dalo slowly reached for Palryma's hand and began to move forward very cautiously. No sooner than they stepped inside did they realize at once that fear and trepidation had no place inside this cave. The dwelling was large enough for a family and the burning fire in the hearth gave a warm and welcoming glow to their new living quarters. The furnishings were handsome, sturdy and plentiful. Tables and chairs lined the walls and bundles of mistral branches lay before the fire. Shelves on the walls held plates and bowls and an elevated alcove nestled one comfy looking sleeping area — another waited for one of the weary travelers in the corner near the fire. In the center of the cave was a massive, long table made of rock. In the middle of the table were neatly laid out tools of different shapes and sizes and, presently, of no discernable meaning to Palryma. But it was clear to Dalo that this is where young Palryma would learn to make the chalices. In this cave, and no other, would he learn the ways of the chalice maker?

"Dalo — where did all these things come from? Did you place them here?"

"No Pallie. Lumpty-shoo-ra! How could I have carried that big rock table in here? Are you cralee-hoo? No, it was not me at all. This must be Batoowa's doing. Oh yes, of this I am very certain. Pallie, it is clear to me that the chalice makers in your line possess a very powerful and giving magic indeed. What we see with our own eyes is the truth of that! Look around you. There is care and giving in all we see. I think they have planned all of this out very well...and may I add, for a very long time. What a graceful place this is!"

"It's as though I was born to be here." said Palryma "There is a calmness about me that was not around as we walked through the forest. I feel as though I have seen this very cave before. But that is not possible, is it Dalo?"

"I think that from this moment forward, Pallie, anything is possible!" Palryma did not respond. He could only stare with his violet eyes at Dalo and smile so broadly that his whole face was alite. "What are you doing?" questioned Dalo. Palryma still did not speak. Nothing on him moved except that his smile grew even broader. "Stop staring at me, Pallie. I don't think that is very polite." Palryma raised his hand to point at Dalo's head and finally spoke. "Your hair, Dalo! In the back of your head! Look at your hair.....that big orange patch in the middle is gone! It has turned to black!" Dalo spun around faster than a twizzle trying to look at the back of his head. "Min-lee-a-too, Pallie...help me here. Help me look at it! Are you certain? Is some of the orange gone??!"

"Stop spinning around like that. You are making me dizzy. You are never going to be able to see the back of your own head! Maybe you are the one who is cralee-hoo! But you must take it on my word and faith that the spot that was once orange is now black."

"Is all the orange gone? Has it really turned all black?"

"No. Not all of it. There is still a good bit of orange left. But that big patch in the back of your head is gone. It turned black right before my eyes!

"Oh by rolly-toe Pallie...this is a wonderful place this cave we are in. Oh free-tooly nigh...I must be a good guide after all. That was the promise, you know. I think I told you that, didn't I? If I was a good guide, Batoowa promised me all of my hair would turn black again." Dalo was beside himself with excitement. "I sing praises of Sweet Lenora-ga for this. I really do!"

Palryma crouched down in front Dalo and took both of his tiny hands into his. "You are the best guide Dalo....the only guide I want.....ever. I would not be here....could not be here if it were not for you. You are my guide."

"Oh limminney-lumpty shoo! This is going to be fun, Pallie. You and me. This surely will be fun."

"Why don't you have a seat at that table next to the wall and I will fill two bowls with clear water from the brook. You have been walking a long way and should rest. Open the cloth wrapping my parents gave me this morning...I'll bet there is something to eat in there."

Palryma walked out of the cave with two bowls and sauntered over to the brook. "This is a very magical place, indeed." he mused as bent down on his knees to scoop up some water. Just as he did, three gold brook fish jumped up and did a dance on their tail fins. "Hi. Hi. Hi." they all said in unison. "Hi there. Hi. How are you?" Palryma fell back on to the seat of his pants and dropped the bowls. "Aren't you going to say 'Hi' to us? We said Hi to you! We have been listening to everything and we had a great idea...we thought it would be great if we can call you Pallie, too?" Palryma was shocked into silence. "Don't you want to say Hi right now? Ok...maybe later then. We have to say Goodbye now! We have to jump back underneath the water...so...Goodbye. Goodbye. Goodbye." they said, again in unison.

Palryma quickly filled the bowls with water and ran back inside the cave. "Dalo! The fish here speak!" His bemused guide was still trying unsuccessfully to have a look at the back of his head to cast an eye on his new spot of black hair. "Sorry Pallie...what was it that you said?"

"I said the fish in the brook...the gold colored ones....they speak! And they dance as well.... on top of the water!"

"Hmmmm" replied Dalo "then they are clearly not for eating! We'll have to get our food some other way." Palryma noticed that the cloth wrapping his parents handed him before he left this very morning had not been opened by Dalo. "Well, as long as you seemed unimpressed with talking fish, I'll have a look in here and see if Mother packed any surprises for us." The knot was easily untied and the contents revealed three sweet couldas and four smooth stones. Looking at them made Palryma miss his parents "I feel like I have not seen them in ten years." He picked up one of the treats and offered it to Dalo, who was still mightily pre-occupied. "Oh...how very nice....sweet couldas! You know Pallie, I really enjoyed the ones we ate at the bakery of Bethnee and Beeloma."

"They brought silver trays full of them to the wedding celebration last night. I think these are only the three that were not eaten by the guests."

"Four."

"No Dalo, Mother packed us three sweet couldas and

Father slipped in four smooth stones in the cloth sack...just for old memories sake."

"Pallie.....I have one sweet coulda in my hand that I am eating with great pleasure, as you can obviously see and there are three left sitting on the cloth next to the stones."

Palryma looked very suspiciously at the cloth. Indeed, Dalo had made the count correctly. Even though he had passed one sweet coulda to his guide, there were still three left! "Dalo, I don't understand this. I am certain that there were but three here when I opened the cloth sack. Perhaps my eyes are playing tricks on me or I am a bit tired from our forest journey."

"Well...whatever it is you should have something to eat. Pick one and swallow it with some of this fresh brook water. It's quite delicious!" Palryma reached for a sweet coulda and almost bit into it but his jaw froze. He waved his hand at Dalo who was chomping away and still trying to pull his hair in front of himself. He looked up long enough to see Palryma waving madly and pointing at the table. He was holding the sweet coulda in his hand and gesturing like a whippet man possessed. "If you don't hurry up and eat that one Pallie...I am going eat all rest of them myself!" Then Dalo saw that Palryma actually was holding an already-bitten-into sweet coulda in his hand yet there were still three more left on the table. Something was amiss with the count.

"By rolly-toe...I know what is going on here! I heard this whispered about when I was in the Big Marsh. Goolie-rah-so-beeno, I never thought I'd see this!! I never thought I'd live long enough to see this carry-on! By rolly-toe, Pallie....this is the Legend of Replacement!! That is what we are seeing with our very eyes in our new home. The Legend of Replacement! Happening right before us!"

"Explain this to me Dalo....for this looks like un-careful magic to me. I think it is upsetting to be around un-careful magic. There was always a rumor that un-careful magic ruled the land in Latima. I was always taught to avoid it as a child. All of my friends were also taught the same. Un-careful magic was not accepted in our village."

Dalo explained that what they had just witnessed was not the same as un-careful magic at all. "There is no need to be alarmed, Pallie." He explained that the Legend of Replacement was a rare gift from Sweet Lenora-ga. It was sometimes presented to people on a great journey. As long as they took only what they needed to survive on the journey, they would want for nothing. "This is a great sign, Pallie. Can you see that? This means that not only are all the chalice makers in your line watching over you as you begin to learn the ways of a Chalice Maker, but Sweet Lenora-ga herself has taken an interest in your training! Oh Pallie...we will want for nothing on this journey....you and me.....we have only to do our jobs... me as the guide and you as the chalice maker."

"What does this mean...take only what you need?" Dalo tried to make Palryma understand that there were many bounties in the land and it would remain so but only if people agreed that they must only take what they need to survive. "There must be something left for those who come behind us, Pallie. It only makes sense, does it not? The land can replenish itself given time."

"Then why are we being presented with this legend?"

Dalo did twenty-three spins in the air and landed on his face. "Do you see what you have done Pallie? You have made me spin too many times in the air! I think I must learn to explain things better."

Palryma crouched down to help his guide off the floor. 'I didn't mean to make you spin like that Dalo." he said as he patted the floor dust from Dalo's jacket. "I was merely asking a question. My father always taught me as a hunter to bring home only what we needed for the day and my mother was always after me to share what I had with my friends. I don't think it's a question of my ever wanting to take too much from the land."

"But we will not be here forever Pallie. Your training will end one day and while it is in the process, we do not have to give a thought to our needs to survive. Sweet Lenora-ga has now seen to that."

"We cannot eat sweet couldas every day! Our teeth will fall out!"

"My very point, Pallie. If you try to eat too many, the replacement will stop. Take only what you need. It will be the same for the delicious tasting water from the brook. You will soon see that the Legend of Replacement will be most helpful and encouraging to both of us as we get the training under way. Now, finish your sweet coulda and head for your sleeping area. We will begin well-rested and fresh tomorrow morning. I am going to take the sleeping area over in the corner by the fire so that I do not have to climb up that ladder to the bigger one. My fat feet and wiggly toes were not meant to climb ladders!

Dalo was asleep in seconds and Palryma was left at the table to ponder the wonder of the Legend of Replacement. He took two of the smooth stones into his hand and rubbed them. "I wish you were here Father.....I feel so confused already and it's only been one day." He took the stones with him as he climbed the ladder to his sleeping area.

"I see you and I hear you, young Palryma. I see you and I hear you." It was the voice of Sweet Lenora-ga but neither the snoring Dalo nor the sleeping Palryma could hear it.

Chapter Eight

The new morning symphony of the Kura birds atop the opening of the Chalice Maker's cave brought the sleepy-eyed Palryma to a wakened state. His stretching and yawning were brought to an abrupt end when he heard the beckoning of Dalo just outside the cave. "Come on Pallie. It's time to get things underway. You have much to learn."

In no time Palryma was ready and standing in front of his guide. The chorus of gold-colored fish in the brook greeted him even more enthusiastically than yesterday. "I've already told them that they could call you "Pallie". It seemed to please them to no end. They are very entertaining fish! Definitely not for eating though!" howled Dalo. Palryma gave a small smile and a slight wave to the fish in the brook.

"Oh...Hi...Hi...Hi Pallie!! We hope you had a beauty-fine sleep! We can't wave back to you because we don't have any arms! Just fins! OK....now we have to jump back into the water!" With that exultation complete, the glee of the fish carried them back into the swirling waters of the brook. Palryma scooped up a bowl full of clear water and eyed the fish at play. "I suppose the Kura birds here speak as well!"

"Not a word, as far as I know!" said Dalo "but they make the most beautiful music I have ever heard from any birds. Did you hear them this morning?"

"Yes...yes I did. It was as if it was music for a new dawning....they seemed like a thousand birds chirping all at once." Palryma sipped his water and let a moment of this new day pass before asking Dalo "What shall we do today?"

Dalo motioned for Palryma to follow him along the dirt and root path leading to the other side of the gulley. "Today, Pallie, we will gather the very large rocks that will eventually take the shape of your first chalices. We will need a half dozen or so. You can carry a few in your arms and the others I will roll back to the cave with my big fat feet!"

Palryma thought this to be an odd way to begin his lessons and figured to be back in the cave within the hour. Dalo, however, proved to be very selective when it came to approving the big rocks. Some were too jagged, others were too dark. A few were too soft and did not possess chalice potential. It was hours and hours before Palryma held up a big rock that Dalo finally approved of. "It's perfect Pallie" shouted his guide. "It's a very good eye you have for rocks!"

"A good eye, you say?" Palryma shouted back "I have been picking up big rocks for hours and hours and this is the first one you like!"

"And look how beautiful it is! Lesson number one Pallie is that perfection is possible in all things. However, it is never possible without patience. Patience and perfection, Pallie. They always go hand in hand. All chalice makers know that!... and now you do, as well! Keep looking...we still need a few more big rocks."

Palryma remembered his vow to his parents not to be headstrong and to listen to the instructions of his guide. "Very well, Dalo. I will not stop until we have what we need."

The hunt continued on until a second beautiful rock and then a third were found. The fourth rock, however, was huge and Dalo was very pleased with his discovery. "Roll this into the dirt and root path, Pallie, please. This one right here is big enough to make two chalices! The huge rock was peppered with blue and pink spots throughout and its colors almost sang out loud when it was placed in the bright sunlight. "It is really quite a beautiful rock indeed, Dalo. It seems that you have a fine eye for rocks yourself!"

"Just luck, Pallie. Only luck for Dalo! I am here to help you — not the other way around."

They both agreed that with the lucky find of the fourth massive rock, which would really serve as two, they could begin their journey back to the cave if they could just locate one more. The sun had long since passed high overhead and might soon travel out of sight. The burden of heavy rocks would make the trip back to the cave longer than the one which brought them to this spot and both wanted to be home before the sky's soft color of pink and orange appeared.

"Try that patch of flowers down there Pallie. See if any nice rocks lay about there."

"I don't see where you mean, Dalo. Where are you pointing?

Dalo repeated his gesture. "Just down there at the end of this turn. You can see a patch of forgetful flowers there....just at the turn of the path. I will wait here for you as my fat feet are beginning to tire."

Dalo rested against the big blue and pink spotted rock and watched the chalice maker head for the patch of forgetful flowers. "I will show him the Legend of Molten Hands when we return to the cave" he said to no one. "I do think, though, that Pallie is showing signs that he will be a very quick learner. Perhaps my time will not be long." Dalo closed his eyes in reflection for a moment and did not notice that

Palryma was waving wildly towards him. It was only the shouts that focused his attention on the new chalice maker. "Dalo....come here quickly." he shouted "there is a bird here in the flower patch....I think he is dead...or nearly so!" Dalo quickly flipped himself twenty times down the path until he landed directly next to Palryma, who was pointing at the bird lying beneath the patch of forgetful flowers. Neither of them could detect the nearly undetectable shallow, almost invisible breathing of the bird. Palryma was correct. This bird was nearly dead.

"Pick him up Pallie. Let's have a closer look at him. Be gentle for if he is still alive we do not want ourselves to be the cause of his death."

Palryma knelt down and carefully placed the bird in his hands. "He has the color of all the rocks we rejected today.... its a very uninviting color of gray, is it not Dalo? How would you agree with me on that?"

"That awful color of gray, Pallie....that is the color of death. That's why I rejected all those rocks. A chalice cannot be the color of death. But this bird surely has that look about him."

"Look here Dalo! This bird is missing a claw. By the very look of the wound, it appears to have been lost in a battle...as though it were ripped right off of him. What a terrible sight this animal is....how sad."

It was then that both Dalo and Palryma saw that the bird was trying with whatever soul was left in him to open one of his eyes. "This bird still lives, Pallie!"

"How can this be so? His feathers are the color of death, he is missing a claw and his eyes are nearly closed shut." Dalo shrugged and moved to make a closer inspection. "There is no doubt but that this bird still lives, Pallie. Whatever he has been though.....whatever battle he has fought against an evil so great who would severe his claw.....this bird still has some will to live."

"I will take him back with us to the cave and help him restore his health!" declared Palryma. "It will not interfere with my training, will it Dalo? Surely we cannot abandon him to certain death among these forgetful flowers, can we? It is too cruel a fate. We must help him."

"You must make this choice Pallie, not I. Clearly we cannot carry all of our beautiful rocks, which are quite heavy, and this bird all the way back to the cave. The rocks are for the chalices and you are a chalice maker chosen by the gods. You must decide."

"Then we take this poor, dying bird with us." decided Palryma without hesitation. "If he is left here another day, he will surely die....perhaps he might die anyway, but I will not leave him here to die alone. With the help of Sweet Lenora-ga, we can restore him to health Dalo – you and I. The rocks we can leave by the roadside until tomorrow. They suffer no immediate fate. And now that I know you approve of them, I will return here tomorrow morning with the first symphony of the Kura birds and bring them home. How would you agree with me on that?

"It is your decision Pallie and I abide it. You seem well pleased with it and that is good. May I add something to it though?" Palryma nodded. "Why don't we roll the massive blue and pink spotted rock back together, for you will not be able to do that tomorrow and carry the other rocks as well. I can push the rock along a bit with my big fat feet and you can help guide it with a free arm as you cradle the bird. That way we will get back together before the night falls and tend to our new bird with some fresh water from the brook. How would you agree with me on that?"

Palryma laughed as he rose with the dying bird in his arm. "I would have to agree with you in every way possible, Dalo. You are very wise, indeed."

Dalo stayed silent but thought this very thought "You are the one who is very wise Pallie, for you have chosen compassion, love and kindness before your own advancement in training to be a chalice maker. You will be one of the great ones. No doubt."

Together they guided and pushed the big rock back along the very dirt and root path that brought them to the dying bird, Settela. Even though neither Palryma nor Dalo recognized him, in the arms of his former rival, Settela was comforted. He was barely aware of his forest surroundings much less any understanding of the chalice-making cave where he was headed. He was unrecognizable now that the bright yellow color of his feathers had turned to deathly gray. He was limp with one claw and thin and battered from injury. But he knew who rescued him and in whose arms he rested. He could not speak and did not know if he would ever be able to speak again. In fact, he did not know if he would be able to live through the night. All he knew was that he was not lying in the patch of forgetful flowers and that every step Palryma took along the dirt and root path took him one step further away from the Castle of Hurrah III and the man who tried to kill him. "I will never forget that evil man" Settela silently vowed "just as I will never forget the kindness of this rescue and my rescuers. I am indebted to them now. If I live, I will prove my worth to them. This I vow."

Settela passed into a slumber while faintly hearing the whistle of one of Palryma's walking songs being thumped out by Dalo. "This is a good sound" he thought "it is the sound of kindness."

Dalo could see that they were finally approaching the cave and said "Say, Pallie....what shall we call this bird? We will have to have a name for him so we can introduce him to the talking fish!"

"Yes. You are right again Dalo. It would be impolite not to introduce him to our talking fish." Palryma looked at the sleeping bird in his arm and said "I think we shall call him "Bird"...just that ...nothing more. Bird. I think it says everything about him that we need to know...and easy for the fish to pronounce, I might add!!!"

"Then Bird it is!...and Bird it shall be. I hope we get to know him well."

"With the help of Sweet Lenora-ga we will, Dalo."

The dimming glow of embers from the fire's warmth and the crisp morning chirping from the Kura birds were signals to Dalo that a new day in the chalice maker's cave had arrived. As he rose from the nestle of his mattress bed of forest leaves and moss, Dalo glanced towards his young chalice maker. "It is good that he sleeps so well. It's a sign of a good heart and a clear mind. I will leave him to it for a while yet and step outside to see what the day has brought." Before pushing open the cave door, Dalo stopped to look upon Bird. "Also a good sign that he made it through night" he said with great thanks. "What horror this poor bird must have suffered. If anyone can restore him to good health, it will be Palryma. What an interesting element he will be in the training of this new chalice maker!" Dalo could only accept that the gods of chalice making must have had a reason to place Bird in Palryma's path.

A treasure chest of forest beauty welcomed Dalo to the new day. Every bloom was alive with special colors and intoxicating scents. The sky was so clear that it seemed endlessly high. The water from the brook sparkled with a cool invitation for Dalo to quench his thirst again and again. And the sweet air was nothing less than a special gift-wrapped present to his lungs. Dalo closed his eyes in giving thanks to all who brought him here with Palryma. "I am truly blessed." he whispered. Dalo's thanksgiving was interrupted by the sudden jumping chorus of the gold-colored fish from the brook. "Hi Dalo! Hi! Hi!" they shouted in their welcoming unison. "We know about the bird already! What's his name? Can we name him! OK – we have to jump back into the water now and then we will come up with a name later! OK. Bye Dalo. Bye. See you later!" And with that the fish were under water as quickly as they were above it. Too quickly as they were to soon learn. When they popped up again later, Dalo had to inform them that while "Fred" certainly might be a nice name for the recovering bird altogether, Palryma had already named him "Bird", and so Bird it was to be. "OK Dalo. OK! Bird it will be. We can name the next one Fred. It will be Bird and Fred and they will be bird brothers! OK. See you later!" And again, the fish were quickly underwater and nearly out of sight. Dalo just shook his head in wonderment. "Who ever heard of a bird named Fred, anyway?" he mused. "I wonder how they already knew about Bird anyway. These are quite unusual fish, I must say."

Dalo walked back into the cave with a bowl of cool water for Bird and one for Palryma. He lifted Bird's head ever so gently so that the just-now-waking bird could swallow. With half a swollen eye opening, he seemed to want to say "Thank you" but neither words nor music came from his parched throat. Dalo was quite sensitive to this and said "Do nothing, Bird, except drink the cooling water. Soon enough you will have strength." Bird managed another two swallows before laying his head to rest again.

"Good morning Dalo!" said Palryma "I surely did sleep a long while – did I not?" Dalo smiled and nodded. "How is Bird?" he asked. "He made it through the night – for that we can be grateful." replied Dalo. Palryma reached over to stroke the tattered feathers and examine Bird for any injury they did not spot yesterday. "He seems to be in one piece – barely," observed Palryma. "Perhaps in a few days we can give him some of the too-too-too berries I saw growing nearby after some of his strength returns." Dalo agreed that would be a wonderful idea, but for now it would have to be just the cool water from the brook.

"I will bring more water to him later" stated Palryma.

"Fine indeed Pallie but if the fish see you, remind them that this bird's name is not Fred!" Palryma gave Dalo a quiz-zacle look "Fred?" "What kind of name is that for a bird?"

"Exactly my point Pallie, but you know how those fish are!"

Palryma let the mini-mystery pass and instead smiled at his guide and said 'What shall we do today Dalo?"

"Ah....glad you asked Pallie. Today you will start to make your first chalice. Roll that big huge rock we brought back yesterday into the cave. It's time for your first lesson."

With great enthusiasm, Palryma opened the cave door all the way and the sunshine immediately filled the inside of the cave with every color either of them had ever seen. There was even a ray of orange and black to match Dalo's hair. There were many rays of deep violet to match Palryma's eyes. And among all the hues was a single ray of pure white. Neither Dalo nor Palryma could have guessed that it represented the real and original color of Bird's feathers. It was a sign from Batoowa that Bird was exactly where he was suppose to be. It was a sign of good things to come. Even while he was sleeping, Bird could feel the love.

Chapter Nine

"OK Pallie! Are you ready??"

"Ready as I'll ever be" replied Palryma a bit nervously.

The huge rock that was peppered with blue and pink spots was now resting in the middle of the cave — too big to lift onto the table. Palryma just stared at it wondering how it was ever to become a chalice — or two — or even three. When he was rolling it into the cave he could not help but wonder how he was ever to cut it down to size with the tools that had been awaiting him on the table when they arrived two days ago. "This doesn't make any sense to me, but nothing really has since I was called after in the wet fields. That seems so very long ago."

"What's that Pallie?"questioned Dalo who was obviously relishing the moment of this first chalice-making lesson. "Oh...nothing" said Palryma "I was just wondering what to do next."

"Come sit next to me on this bench and you will see."

The two sat side by side on the bench without speaking. Finally Palryma said, "When does the lesson start Dalo?"

"It already has Pallie."

"The lesson begins with no words or instruction. How am I to learn?"

"What are you thinking Pallie? What is on your mind right this very moment?"

"How to make a chalice out of this huge rock, of course."

""Exactly!! By rolly-toe! That is exactly how the lesson begins."

"I don't understand."

"Crum-de-crum Pallie! You're practically ahead of me and you don't even know it! You are wondering how you are going to make a chalice out of this rock – Yes?"

"That's correct Dalo – I already told you that's what I was thinking."

"Did you have any particular shape in mind at all when you wondered how you would get this chalice made?"

"Well, actually...yes. Yes I did have some idea of a chalice shape."

"Then that's where your lesson starts Pallie! The shape of things to come!! You are deciding that for yourself. The shape of your chalice is the one that you, yourself, decide! Show me!"

"What?"

"Are you just plain cralee-hoo Pallie! I said show me. Trace with your finger on the rock the shape of the chalice you want to make."

Palryma reached over and drew with his index finger a shape.

"By rolly-toe that's quite creative Pallie. It seems like it might make a very nice chalice indeed. I'm glad you did not draw over the whole rock for that might make the chalice way too big."

Palryma smiled but still seemed quite bewildered. "So..... now what?"

"So now, young chalice maker, you scoop out the part of

the rock that will become your first chalice and place it on the work table."

"Scoop it out, Dalo?" Is that what you said? With what may I ask?"

Without missing a beat, Dalo replied "With your hands, of course. Your chalice making hands."

"Now who's cralee-hoo!" laughed Palryma. "How do you expect me to scoop out a piece of this huge rock with my hands?"

Dalo looked at Palryma deeply and spoke only these words "Like this." The former forest schwimmy, now appointed guide to the land's new chalice maker then reached out with both his hands and dug into the huge rock as though it were no more than a big clump of soft earth in the forest. He got up from the bench and placed the piece of rock on the work-table. Palryma was frozen in place as though he simply could not move — as though he simply could not believe what he had just seen. Dalo turned about with a smile so wide it was making his long earlobes wiggle. And another clump of his hair had just turned completely black. "Now it's your turn Pallie!"

Palryma looked at his hands and shook his head "I can't...I...haven't....I..."

"Of course you can, Pallie. You are a Chalice Maker and this is how chalice making begins!"

"But my hands....they don't..."

"Oh lumpty shoo ra na!" exclaimed Dalo "I got so excited about your first lesson I forgot to tell you about the Legend of Molten Hands. Sorry about that Pallie."

"The Legend of Molten Hands??"

"Yes! Yes! By rolly-toe! It's the legend! All new chalice makers get molten hands. You can go through rocks....anything.....

trees....you name it...as long as it's being done in pursuit of chalice making! Isn't that just crickey-krackey! You've had them since the very day of your initiation in the wet fields. Only I forgot to tell you until just now.....not that it would have made any sense to you until now, but that's beside the point. You have them. All chalice makers have them. So go ahead...scoop away!

"You scooped part of the rock out with your hands Dalo. Are you secretly a chalice maker? Is that why you are my guide?"

"Ach....la-de-do-me-rah Pallie! I have already explained to you why I am your guide."

"Scoop out some more rock for me!"

"Nope...no can do my friend. Batoowa just let me show it to you once. You are the one who has the magic — the Legend of Molten Hands — not me. In fact, I'll never be able to do it again — so I hope you were watching closely. Now go ahead — scoop out that part of the rock that you traced on earlier."

Palryma's head was spinning from the legend and from what he had just watched Dalo do. He kept looking from the rock to his hands — back and forth — from the rock to his hands. He finally took a huge breath and reach slowly for the rock with both of them. With his eyes wider than saucers of the Millooley Star, his strong hunter's hands slid smoothly into the huge rock and scooped out the part he had traced upon for his first chalice.

"I did it!!" he screamed. "I did it Dalo!!" "Look — I have the rock in my hands!"

Dalo pointed wildly at the table — gesturing for Dalo to place it there — next to his. He twirled eleven times in place and began to thump about the cave with his big fat feet. "This is a good day, Pallie!! This is a really good day! Look how well you did with your first lesson! Why you reached right in there like you were born to make chalices, by rolly-toe!! Just like you were born to make them!!"

Palryma, too, began to leap about the cave. He was smiling, singing, and whistling his favorite walking song "One Love for Me". "That was more fun than hunting!! I never thought I would say that, Dalo because I missed my bow and arrows so....but what I just did...that was more fun than hunting!!"

Dalo roared with laughter as he watched Palryma beam with joy. "Yes...I think you are well on your way, young chalice maker....well on your way indeed." His silent observation was cut short when Palryma pointed to the small bed of leaves they made for Bird. "Look Dalo! I think Bird is moving!"

"Moving" was a bit of an exaggeration, but it was obvious that Bird was attempting to lift his head somewhat – perhaps to see what all the merriment in the cave was about. Palryma moved closer to him and instinctively reached to stroke his feathers but then reared back immediately. "I won't harm him with my molten hands will I Dalo?"

"You didn't harm him yesterday or this morning and you had the molten hands then, too. Today was just the first day you used them. I think Bird will survive your touch!"

Palryma crouched over the rescued bird and began to gently stroke his feathers. "Welcome to the Chalice Maker's cave, Bird. I hope you will be happy here. My name is Palryma. And then he came closer to Bird to whisper "And that fine looking gentleman over there is called Dalo. Dalo it is and Dalo you must call him...not Dallie, not Dalo-boy and certainly not Mr. Dalo. Just Dalo. He is my guide. I am a chalice maker and Dalo is my guide....the finest guide there ever was."

Bird tried to open his swollen eye all the way but it was

not ready yet. He tried to eek out an acknowledging nod with his head but it was all he could do to rest it down again on the leaves. But in his weak heart he knew that he was among friends now and well protected. And for that, he was easily the most grateful, if not the happiest one in the cave of the chalice maker.

For the next few hours they worked hand in hand like two expert surgeons — the chalice maker and his guide. Palryma would scoop out shapes of rock for chalices and Dalo would line them up on the worktable readying them for further shaping. As Palryma scooped out the shape, Dalo would chip away at it with the table tools. They whistled while they worked and chatted about the new life of a chalice maker. Palryma had many questions and Dalo helped as much as he could but explained that a lot of the answers would come to Palryma by and by. "Live the life, Pallie and you will soon see the answers on your own." advised Dalo. "Never abuse your powers as a chalice maker and you will find yourself forever protected by Sweet Lenora-ga."

Some of Dalo's advice sunk in with Palryma and some he did not bother to ponder presently as he was absolutely consumed with his new molten hands and the beginning shapes of his new chalices. "I think we are doing quite well here Dalo. How would you agree with me on that?!"

"I would agree that you still have to return to the dirt road and bring back the rocks we left behind yesterday." chortled Dalo. "They were quite beautiful and will also make nice chalices. What we have here is surely not the end of the line. No! by rolly-toe! It is only the beginning."

"Oh...of course — you are correct. I forgot about those two rocks we left behind. I think it will be a good idea if I take a walk now and get them. You can rest here with Bird. I'll get some of the too-too-too berries on my way back just in case Bird starts to feel better later today or tomorrow. At least we'll have something ready for him."

"Excellent idea that you have there Pallie! I will take a rest and put my fat feet and wiggly toes in the swirling brook for fun until you return!"

Palryma brushed his hands off and grabbed a sackcloth above the fire's hearth. "I won't be too long." he said as he placed a very light kiss on Bird's head as he passed him by. "And I'll have some sweet too-too-too berries for you when you wake, Bird." When he stepped outside the gold brook fish were waiting for him. "Hi Pallie! Hi. Hi. Hi! How are you and your molten hands? Do you want to cool them off in our swirling brook? You can if you want to. The water is very cool! How is Fred's brother?! OK. We have to jump back in the water now!" Palryma shouted to them below the water "His name is Bird!!" He was going to continue but realized that it would be useless "They won't stop until I bring home another bird and name him Fred." Heading down the road away from the cave he realized that this was the first time he had been all on his own since that special day of his calling in the wet fields. It was a funny feeling he decided. "I used to spend so many hours alone hunting and now I am constantly in some-one's company. This life of a Chalice Maker surely will be a different one!" Characteristically abandoning a wondering thought, Palryma began to whistle his favorite walking song "One Love for Me" until he saw the rocks that he and Dalo laid by the side of the dirt road. Then he stopped. But not because he spotted the rocks.

Because he saw *her.*

Chapter Ten

Palryma was not more than 30 feet from the two rocks that he had to bring back to the cave. He stopped whistling immediately upon seeing her because his jaw dropped. He stood as though frozen in time and blinked his eyes twice. He tried to step closer to the rocks but he felt like his boots were stuck in the dirt road. Was it a mirage? If it was not, he thought it was nothing less than the singularly most beautiful girl he had ever seen. She did not notice him as her back was turned and she seemed to be collecting sweet forest flowers in her straw basket. She moved like a graceful breeze and had long, long flaxen hair that followed every lithesome turn and bend she made. Her gown was a royal color of rose and he was just close enough to hear her humming some sort of song. Then he saw her face.

He wanted to collapse but feared an eventual embarrassment. She had night sky blue doe-like eyes set on either side of a tiny, sculpted nose, shaped and held in place with skin the color of a white and whispy, morning cloud. The humming of her forest song was coming through lips that could not have begged to be redder if they tried. Her eyelashes could have scooped up Palryma's heart in one blink. He knew two things in an instant. First, there would never be any way to measure her beauty. Second, this was her! This was the one he whistled about. She was the girl he envisioned in his favorite walking song "One Love for Me". He knew this in his heart and he knew it immediately. "I have met up with her." he whispered ever so quietly "I have finally met up with her." He was nearly bursting apart with joy and wonderment. His violet eyes glistened. He did not know if he should approach her. He knew quite well that in his village, it was always considered so terribly impolite to approach a woman without another villager to make a proper introduction. It was what happened when his father first laid eyes on his mother years ago. Bestra begged Beeloma to make a hurried introduction before Merrilyee disappeared. But for this important moment, Palryma saw no one who could make a proper introduction and he had no time to run back to the cave and grab Dalo. And they were too long a distance from Goosra. He had no choice. He had to act fast before she began to leave. As if by magic, Palryma suddenly remembered the words his father spoke to him after he returned home from his anointing in the wet fields: "The natural order of things no longer applies to you." were Bestra's exact words to his newly appointed son on that day. Right then and there Palryma knew he could introduce himself to this forest beauty. He did not need anyone else. He just had to try and remain calm...or at least appear to be so.

The first few words he spoke had no sound at all. He clearly moved his jaw and parted his lips but nothing came out. He cleared his throat a bit and tried once again.

"Hello and heavens above to you" he said. There was no response from the beautiful forest girl. He tried again — this time a little louder.

"Ahem....I say...hello and heavens above." She turned towards him. Nearly blinded by her beauty, Palryma could feel his lips go dry. But he refused to give up. "It seems you are having a fine day collecting sweet forest flowers. How would you agree with me on that?" The forest girl looked at her basket and then looked back at this stranger in the forest who was addressing her. Still she made no effort at responding. Palryma moved a step closer and pointed this time at her basket just in case she did not understand. "Your basket there"... he said..."it is quite filled with flowers...have you been here very long? Are you collecting them for a friend?"

She finally spoke "I collect them for one who is close to me." Palryma thought her voice sounded just like honey tasted. Rich and pure and sweet. He was trying to think of something else to say but his brain pounded inside with gigantic echoes of nothing. He clasped his hands in front of him at chest level. "Whoever it is that you collect these flowers for is a very lucky one indeed...by rolly-toe!" No sooner was Dalo's favorite exclamation out of his mouth than Palryma wanted to disappear into the sky. "Oh no" he thought only to himself "why am I talking the silly language to this unspeakably beautiful girl?"

"By what?" she said "Rolley's Toes?" She seemed very wary of Palryma. "I have never heard of that before. Is that a polite manner of addressing someone? May I ask where you are from?" she said as she took several steps backwards.

"Oh my....it's is nothing" he stuttered "I mean it is simply an expression a friend of mine uses when he is excited and I am very excited right now...."

The forest girl interrupted him. "Pardon me, I don't mean to be impolite but why are you excited? I mean what exactly has got you so excited that you would use such an expression."

Palryma was digging a hole and he knew it but he did not know how to stop. "I am very excited about you! I mean you are very exciting to me." By this time he was dreading the fact that he even had a voice at all. But he went right on. "I mean... I see you and I get excited...well really just in my dreams of course...that is up until now. I mean now that I see you I am really excited!" The forest girl turned and started to walk away very quickly. Palryma held his hands to the back of his head and shouted "Oh please...don't run away. I just wanted to meet you! I'll stop being excited!" She did not look back. Palryma's heart was sinking fast and without so much as a thought he began to chase after the forest girl. She started to run and in doing so dropped her basket of sweet forest flowers. Palryma ran as fast as he could down the dirt road so as to be a good bit ahead of her. Then he cut into the forest and stood at least a good few feet ahead of her. He held his hands up and spoke with a strong voice "I beg of you, my lady. Please don't run. I mean no harm. I ask only for an introduction. I am far from my village and there is no one to assist me. Please." The forest girl stopped but still had an uneasy look on her face. "Please let me pass sir," she said with an ever so slight quiver in her lower lip.

"Again...my lady...you are in no danger" he said trying to be re-assuring. "Allow me to bow before you." And so he did – the Chalice Maker – and quite gallantly. He rose out of the courtly bow with his palms outstretched. "If you please, my lady. My name is Palryma. I am the son of Bestra and Merrilyee and I hail from the village of Goosra. I walk this land now 23 years."

The forest girl relaxed somewhat, eased by Palryma's gesture but did not let down her guard. "Goosra is far from this place in the forest, sir. What brings you so far from your home?"

Palryma beamed at the chance to say "I am the new Chalice Maker, my lady and I am here in this part of the forest with my guide Dalo, who is teaching me the ways of a chalice maker. We have our cave just a little ways down this dirt road." He waited for a reaction but none came. "I have been making chalices all the morning with Dalo. I think we are doing quite well!"

She looked at him very strangely. Her face seemed more relaxed but she bore a little suspicious countenance now. "A chalice maker, you say?"

"Yes!" Palryma with pride. "I have only just received my powers a few days ago! He paused for a moment to see if his announcement would draw out some enthusiasm from this newfound beauty. Sadly, none came. So he continued, some-what sheepishly. "Did you not hear that there was a new chalice maker in the land?"

"I heard some of this kind of talk, but I paid it no mind as I have other concerns at the moment."

Palryma humbled himself for a moment. "Of course... what would the news of a chalice maker bear upon your life? Surely, as you say, you have some other concerns. I hope these concerns serve you well my lady." Palryma strode well wide to her side and went over to pick up her basket of flowers. He stretched his arm way, way out to return it to her. "It seems as though I caused some of them to fall out because you thought you had to run from me — may I help replace them for you? I will walk on the dirt road and you can stay here — a safe and polite distance." The forest girl began to smile and Palryma almost fainted. It was a most warm and welcoming smile. Just as he imagined it might be. "Thank you kindly sir. I accept your offer. There is a lovely and fresh cache of sweet forest flowers just over there." They picked the flowers in silence as Palryma could not think of another word to say but only hoped that he did not fall over. The forest girl knew she was with someone special but was too shy to speak her heart. When the basket was full to the brim of new flowers they looked at each other, neither knowing exactly what to say.

Finally, Palryma broke the sentimental silence. "May I please know your name, my lady?"

"My name is Allura Rose" she replied softly.

"It's a beautiful name. A perfect name for you, if you do not consider that comment impolite."

"Not at all. I am quite happy with it," she laughed. "But, I must be going now. My grandmother is unwell and always looks forward to a nice collection of sweet forest flowers each day from me to give her cheer."

"My name is Palryma."

"Yes...so you said. Palryma the Chalice Maker – from Goosra."

Palryma scratched his head in the recollection of his earlier introduction. "Yes...you are right...I already did say that. Umm...so you collect flowers every day?"

"Yes."

"Every day...right here in this section of the forest...each day?...so with the grace of Sweet Lenora-ga, you will be here again tomorrow collecting flowers....perhaps at about the very same time?"

"Yes, that is true" said Allura Rose "I will be here again tomorrow."

"That is such a coincidence! I myself will be here tomorrow collecting rocks for my chalices! What a wonderful coincidence! So I will see you tomorrow then?

"Yes, Palryma. You will see me tomorrow."

Palryma bowed again. "Well, until then. Safe home, Allura Rose. Safe home."

Allura Rose headed towards the forest glen and Palryma

walked swiftly back towards cave whistling his favorite walking song "One Love for Me".

By the time he reached the cave, Palryma was in a full out run. He nearly leapt as he screeched to a halt in front of Dalo who was lazily paddling his fat feet and wiggly toes back and forth in the brook. Next to him lay Bird, who was brought outside by Dalo as he thought some sunshine and fresh air would do him good and ease his recovery. It seemed to be working as Bird was carefully propped up in his makeshift nest with his eyes open — not fully opened but opened enough to watch his rescuer, Palryma, jump and twirl in the air with glee.

"I met her, Dalo!! I actually met her!" he said with unabounding joy. "I cannot begin to describe how beautiful she is...and we spoke...actually spoke...and we gathered some sweet forest flowers and...." Dalo interrupted him.

"Lumpty-too-na-ree Pallie!! Calm down or you will scare the fish!" He looked at the young chalice maker with bewilderment. "Who did you meet? Who has you nearly doing air twizzles right before my eyes!"

Palryma took a deep breath before he made his announcement. "Her name is Allura Rose and I will see her again tomorrow in the forest."

Dalo pondered this possibility and wondered what to make of it. He made a quick but quiet thought to himself. "This is an unexpected hitch in the lesson plans, but I will have to see what comes of this new development. Pallie seems to be glowing from the inside out at the moment, so I will adjust our chalice making progress somewhat. I am certain that Batoowa will understand." Then he addressed Palryma directly. "I assume, Pallie, that after you meet up again with this forest beauty and come home tomorrow, you will not forget to return with the rocks!"

Only then did Palryma realize his transgression and profusely apologized on the spot. "Oh no! I am very, very sorry Dalo. That was terrible of me. I was right next to the rocks when I saw her and everything just seeped out of my brain. I could only think of her. I will go back right now and collect the rocks."

"And the too-too-too berries for Bird? Are you hiding them in your pockets?"

Palryma buried his face in his hands. He crouched down and stroked Bird's little head. "I am very sorry Bird. I didn't mean to forget you but she is so beautiful that I felt like I was under some spell. I am leaving right now to get you some berries!" For the first time since he was rescued from under the patch of forgetful flowers, there appeared the tiniest little twinkle in one of Bird's eyes.

"No need for you to return this very moment, Pallie. We have no real, immediate need of the rocks today and the Kura birds kindly gave Bird some of their own breakfast berries...... birds of a feather, you might say....you know how it goes!" Palryma gave a wave of his hand up to the Kura birds sitting atop the entrance to the cave that were, as usual, engaged in symphonic song but acknowledged Palryma's wave with a fluttering of their sapphire colored wings.

"Come sit next to me Pallie! Take off your boots and put your feet in the brook. It feels quite wonderful. I will move my fat feet and wiggly toes over so you have room. You can tell me all about this beautiful forest girl named Allura Rose."

Chapter Eleven

Some considerable time passed and the arrival of the evening breezes proved a good indicator at the cave that the
Chalice Maker and his guide would be better off continuing
their conversation inside. Palryma built a fire of mistral wood
and the crackling and sweet scent of its smoke permeated the
room as it floated up the chimney. Dalo busied himself by
eating one of the now never-ending supply of sweet couldas
and picked off a tiny crumb of it to feed to Bird. It was obvious from his devourment that Bird, too, would develop a great
fondness for the creations from the bakery of Bethnee and
Beeloma. Once the fire was self-sustaining, Palryma sat down
at the work table and began to review the shapes and sizes of
the chalices he worked on early that morning. He improved
upon them by running his index finger along the cups and
stems to perfect the chalice shapes. He learned that the magic
of his molten hands could be used to define shapes as well as
scoop them out. Dalo watched him very carefully and thought
"What a quick and sharp learner this one is! It's almost as
though he teaches himself."

"They look like they will become fine chalices Pallie! Very
fine indeed."

"Yes...yes, I will certainly agree with you on that Dalo.
But do you not think that they would be truly fine if we could

add some bit of color to them? I mean the spotted colors in the rock are pretty enough, but there is an odd look of sameness about them even though they are presented in different shapes and sizes. How would you agree with me on this?"

Dalo pondered the question for a moment. He wanted Palryma to make the most beautiful chalices that he could and he wanted them to be a reflection of Palryma's interests and design. He knew his job was not to actually tell Palryma how to make the chalices but rather to show him the best way to make them according to the decisions made by Palryma. In the end, if the decisions made by Palryma were good ones and the chalices were, indeed, quite beautiful then Dalo would have done his job as a good guide...and then he'd have all his black hair back! So, according to Dalo's thinking, the decision was very easy.

"I'd say that I would have to agree with you, Pallie, in every way possible!" He laughed at the sound of himself sounding like a villager from Goosra. Palryma smiled broadly at the thought of it. "What shall we do then?" asked the young chalice maker. "Where do we find some color for these new chalices?"

"Easy as eating bakery pie Pallie," answered Dalo with all the confidence of a good guide. "We will go to the shore-by-the-sea. I am told that there are things there that you have never seen in Goosra. I am told there are things of such brilliant color there — such as you could never imagine! I believe that the new colors you seek to make truly beautiful chalices will be there — right at the shore-by-the-sea!"

Palryma's violet eyes brightened at the suggestion. "I have heard of such a place when I was just a young boy hunter. I have heard that there are animals there that will pop up from the sea and they are bigger than any of the village houses!

I was told by Mikraught, the village tale-teller that it is a place of great mystery. Birds are said to fly down from high in the sky and scoop food right from the water with their claws. Mikraught also told me a tale that I could hardly believe – that there are no trees at this shore-by-the-sea...only bits of tall grass here and there....and that the water can rise higher than three grown hunters before it crashes to the ground. What a sight this must be!

"Well...I think there are a few trees and bushes...not many mind you...but the ones that are there, I think you will find quite useful in your chalice making! And as for the animals that rise from the sea – yes, that is quite right. Palryma was strangely silent which gave Dalo pause. "What's the matter Pallie? I thought you wanted some color for your chalices."

"Yes...of course Dalo...I certainly do want this. It will be a wonderful addition to my learning the ways of a chalice maker." he replied hesitantly. "But you see....well....I sort of promised....I mean I told Allura Rose that I would meet her in the forest tomorrow and I really want to see her again. In fact, I was going to ask you if you would like to come with me as well. I would very much like you to meet her....and perhaps we can bring Bird along with us."

"Ahhh...yes." said Dalo as he stroked his long beard "the forest girl. Musn't forget about her, must we?" Palryma seemed concerned that there might be a conflict and he remembered the promise he made to his father that he would follow the instructions of his guide. But, then again, this was no ordinary girl...this was Allura Rose. He said nothing while Dalo mulled the facts around in his head. What he could not hear was Dalo secretly thinking to himself "It seems that this young beauty has a hold on my new chalice maker. I think she will factor deeply in his training. Best to meet her sooner than later."

"OK Pallie. I think the shore-by-the-sea can wait for a day. If we were to travel there tomorrow we would have to leave even before the first rays of the sun woke the Kura birds and then you would have to miss your meeting with this girl who seems to leave your young heart so pleased. We will meet her tomorrow...all three of us...you and Bird and me. I think Bird will be strong enough to bear a short trip and it might even do him good."

"Thanks Dalo. Thank you most kindly. I just know you will like her! And I can fashion a carrying sack to put Bird in so that he can see everything as we walk along."

"Maybe we will teach him that song you like so much. What's the name of it again? I forget." said Dalo with a sly grin. "Is it "I Love Only One"?...it's something like that, isn't it?"

"You know very well what the name of that song is Dalo! Stop teasing...it's not polite!"

"Tell me again!" Dalo insisted.

"It's called "One Love for Me" and it's my favorite walking song. You know that!"

"Yes...that's it! I knew I would remember it! "One Love for Me"...and so it shall be. We'll have to teach that one to Bird, won't we?"

Dalo walked over to his bed and fell promptly asleep. "I've had a very long day." was the last Palryma heard him say before he nestled in. Palryma stared into the fire for a long while with many thoughts on his mind. He sighed heavily with the realization that as full of change as his life had been over the last few days, there were many, many more to come. Especially now that he had met the girl of his dreams. "I just know I will marry her." he whispered, "I just have to." He slowly pulled Bird's nest closer to him and said "I will teach you that special walking song myself, Bird — just to make sure you get it right! Maybe you would even like to sing it at my wedding!" He stroked Bird's feathers very softly and noticed that the deadly color of gray was fading and a bright and very pure color of white was slowly appearing on some of his feathers. He gave Bird another small crumb of sweet coulda before he picked up one of the table tools and began to chip away at the chalices for his parents. "I'm pretty sure they will like these" he said to no one.

He was so pre-occupied with his work that he did not hear the very quiet and scratchy sound coming from Bird's beak. "Thank you" said Bird. "Thank you." Soon enough Bird, too, was fast asleep.

Palryma continued to chip away for hours shaping the gifts for Bestra and Merrilyee. He thought of all the colors he might be able to add to them from the shore-by-the-sea to make them the most beautiful chalices ever. "I can hardly wait to get there." he said "but not until after I see Allura Rose again."

Outside the cave the Kura birds had long since ended their symphony singing for the day. They sat quietly and motionless atop the cave until one of them said, "When do you think he will finally tell him?"

"I don't know" said another "but it had best be soon or he'll find out on his own."

"And that will not be good. Not at all." said the first Kura bird. They all nodded in agreement.

A small silver slipper of a moon cast only a faint light over the land. The night sky was pin-drop quiet and the motionless air gave impressions that life no longer existed. It was, therefore, most difficult to notice the dark-as-night flying Reelatta horses in the sky. Swooping about and grouped together as they were, one could only imagine what fearsome task was at hand. Their mission was no mystery to them, though. Their orders came from the dark shadow lurking high above the Dusky Hill.....from Hurrah III. "Find me that chalice maker and bring him back to me." he cursed "Do away with the silly guide and if you see Settela, finish him off."

It was only a matter of time before morning came. Tomorrow was another day.

Chapter Twelve

Ominous as the late night might have appeared to be, it was ultimately uneventful as the Chalice Maker's cave remained undiscovered by the dark-as-night flying Reelatta horses and they returned, vanquished for the moment, to the Castle of Hurrah III; before the first new ray of sun returned the waters of the brook outside the cave to their inviting, cool and babbling state.

Dalo was the first to wake inside the cave and he was pleasantly surprised to notice that Bird seemed to be sitting almost upright in his homemade nest. "By rolly-toe Bird! You are looking better every day" he proclaimed. "Soon enough you will be singing with the Kura birds!" Bird wanted to speak.... tried to speak, but still could not find his voice. He could only manage a visible nodding of his head in agreement. He wanted very badly to speak....to explain himself, but it seemed that right now would not be the time for that revelation.

"I am going to fill this cave with sunlight!" cried Dalo as he pulled and tugged at the heavy stone door "and then we are going to wake that young chalice maker and get on with the business of this day. We have a walk into the forest set for ourselves.....rocks to collect and chalices to make and a pretty girl to meet, if we are to believe Pallie!"

"What's that about a pretty girl, I hear?" said Palryma as

he wakened to the sound of Dalo's audible agenda.

"I said we are suppose to meet a pretty girl in the forest, are we not, Pallie?"

"Not to be impolite or to correct you Dalo, but if you will recall, I did not say that she was pretty....I said that she was the most beautiful girl I had ever seen."

"Ah......that you did Pallie....that you did. But how are Bird and I ever to see for ourselves from inside this cave?! Get yourself up and let's get on with this day!"

Palryma leapt down from his lofty sleeping area and plopped himself right next to the spot on the working table where Bird was nested. "What say you Bird? Do you feel up to a walk into the forest?" Again, Bird was able to manage a visible nod but nothing more. "I think Bird is looking very much better this morning, Dalo. How would you agree with me on this?"

"I think Bird would feel a sight better if he had some fresh too-too-too berries. We'll give him some along the way...that is if we ever get out of here!!"

Dalo's hinting admonishment hurried Palryma to prepare a carrying sack to place Bird in, and gather a few sweet couldas from their never-ending supply. He could not help but notice that quite a few more of Bird's feathers had turned a beautiful, pure white overnight. Palryma took this as a sure sign that Bird was well on his way to a full recovery. Bird took it as a sign that he was returning to his old self — the beautiful flying creature that flew happily in the skies above the land before he succumbed to the dark temptations of Hurrah III.....before evil and the promise of power turned him into the talking bird Settela with yellow feathers...a different kind of flying creature altogether. "I will tell him soon." Bird vowed silently "I will tell this kind, young man everything as soon as I find my voice. I will tell him the truth and I pray that he will not cast me out."

Palryma was getting very excited about meeting Allura Rose again and the broad smile on his face was readily apparent to the gold colored brook fish as soon as he walked towards the brook for some water. They leapt from the water immediately. "Hi Pallie! Hi. Hi. Hi. We see you with the big smile! We already know about your girlfriend!! Are you going to kiss her today?? Kiss her once for us!! OK? We have to jump back in the water right now!" And back they went. "Well.....are you?" smiled Dalo.

"Am I what?" said the slightly embarrassed chalice maker.

"Going to kiss the forest girl?"

"Her name is Allura Rose...I told you that already. And you're not suppose to ask me embarrassing questions like that. It's impolite."

"Well....if it's part of your training as a chalice maker, then it wouldn't really be impolite for me to ask now, would it Pallie!?"

Palryma's violet eyes peered at his guide through half-shuttering eye lids "Dalo" he said quite matter-of-factly "kissing pretty girls is not something I need you to train me in as I do not see how it effects my chalice making." Besides" he added dryly "if, in fact, I need any lessons in this kissing matter at all, I would prefer to receive them from the pretty girl I might be kissing, if it's all the same to you!"

"My...my Pallie! You surely must be looking forward to this kiss!" "Are you certain that you want Bird and I to come along with you?"

"Can we please stop talking about kissing, Dalo!? Please ...I am anxious enough about seeing Allura Rose again. And... please don't embarrass me when we get there! I don't know how we got started on this kissing thing anyway."

"Well, Pallie....it really was just a simple question from the fish!"

"Arrggh...those fish!" said Palryma with a dismissive wave "how do they know so much anyway?" He and Dalo, along with Bird in the cloth sack shoulder carrier, began to head down the dirt root path keeping a keen eye in the distance for the beautiful forest girl named Allura Rose.

"Say Pallie....how come you're not whistling that favorite walking song of yours?"

"I can't...I've tried, but my lips have gone dry." he said with a certain disappointment. "Maybe later." he added as he fed Bird another of the too-too-too berries he picked along the way. "Bird surely is fond of those berries, isn't he Pallie? He has quite an appetite for them!"

"It's good to see him eating something besides the small crumbs of sweet couldas. Have you noticed how so many of his feathers are turning such a pretty white?"

"Yes, indeed. That's a sure sign that the color of death is leaving him. He was probably quite a beautiful bird before he was left for dead in those forgetful flowers." mused Dalo. "I sure wish you would whistle a walking song for us, Pallie! My big fat feet and wiggly toes feel like thumping along to something!"

Then they heard it. It was soft at first and only a few notes. But there was no mistaking it.

Bird was beginning to sing!

"Dalo! Did you hear that?" Palryma was stunned. He crouched down so Dalo could peer into the cloth carrying sack. "I think that sound came from Bird!" Dalo's smile was reaching his long ear lobes and his toes were wiggling on their own! "By rolly-toe, Pallie! This is a great day! I think Bird is giving me something for my big fat feet to thump along to!.....

Bird...do you want to see 'ol Dalo thump along to your pretty song?" Bird nodded in agreement. "Give him some more too-too-too berries, Pallie! They seem to bring out the best in him." Palryma fed Bird some more berries, which he relished. Then he began to sing again...a bit louder this time.

"Sweet Lenora-ga!!! He's going to burst with song!! Just listen to that, Dalo! Isn't Bird a beautiful singer!"? Dalo did sixteen flips in the air and then jumped up again in a flurry of violet and white twizzles. "Lumpty-shoo-ra Pallie! Do you hear what Bird is trying to sing?! It's that favorite walking song of yours! How did he know that tune?"

Just as sure as Dalo's hair was black and orange, Bird was definitely eeeking out the Chalice Maker's favorite walking song "One Love for Me".

"I can't believe this!" shrieked Palryma as he fed Bird a couple more berries "how did he know this song?"

"Maybe the gold-colored fish in the brook?" suggested Dalo. "Maybe they taught it to him."

"Those fish know a lot....but they don't know *my* song!" replied Palryma with pride. "I wonder if he heard me whistling it last night after you went to sleep and I was still working on my chalices." Palryma paused for a thought. "That can be the only explanation. If that's the case then Bird, here, is a very intelligent one indeed!"

Dalo realized then that it was clearly no accident that they discovered Bird hidden under the forgetful flowers just a few days before. "There is a real reason why Bird has been sent to be part of this chalice maker's training." Dalo thought as he watched Palryma feed Bird another berry and coax a few more notes from his throat "he will play a significant part for our young chalice maker. What part, though, is yet unclear to me. I will pay very close attention from now on. Very close attention, indeed."

By this time Bird was singing as though he had never stopped. Dalo joined in with the thumping of his big fat feet and the three of them made their way down the dirt root path to look for Allura Rose.

Before the trio had finished their whistling songfest, Palryma's sharp violet eyes saw his vision of loveliness collecting sweet forest flowers in the glen. He stopped in his tracks for a moment to watch her move with grace and walk bathed entirely in sunlight rays that seemed specially matched to the blush in her cheeks.

Dalo tripped slightly at the sudden halt and looked up to see what caused it. "Ah....this must be our girl," he whispered. "Rose and pink rays of the sun, too!! She has definitely got special connections to be graced with special sunlight."

"There she is! Do you see her Dalo?!" beamed Palryma.

"Yes...yes... I see her indeed Pallie for she is the only girl in the glen right now."

"Oh no Dalo...not true....she is the only girl in *the world* right now!!" Bird strained his narrow neck as far up as he could to catch a glimpse of Allura Rose. "Isn't she beautiful, Dalo?"

"She's as beautiful as a forest schwimmy, Pallie. Why don't you lift Bird up a bit so he can see her, too?" When Palryma took Bird out of the carrying sack so he could get a better view he burst into a chirping so sweet that it carried directly down into the glen. Palryma laughed at the Bird's musical appreciation. "I'm glad you approve Bird!"

"Well, let's get a move on down there for proper introductions!" cried Dalo.

Just as they started to move, Allura Rose turned around for she had heard Bird's chirping. It was a moment that changed Palryma's life forever. When he saw her face this time he knew for certain that he would give his heart forever. His was a thought beyond a festive marriage ceremony; his was a thought for eternity. "My life will never be the same from this moment forward. I will become whatever kind of chalice maker I need to be in order to win her heart until the end of time. On the graces of Sweet Lenora-ga, I make this vow." With the simple wave of Allura Rose's hand to say hello, it was as though she waved a magic wand to create a new world for Palryma, son of Bestra and Merrilyee. "Let's step lively, Dalo! It's time for you to meet the one I love!"

Palryma returned the wave and shouted "Hello and heavens above! I have brought some friends for you to meet!" He hastened from a fast walk towards the glen into a trot and Dalo could not keep pace. He chuckled at watching Palryma's bouyant enthusiasm bring him nearer and nearer to Allura Rose. "I'll show him!" he laughed and with that Dalo did 34 flips into the air and landed in the glen amidst a buzz of rose and pink colored twizzles. When Palryma saw this he darted with Bird in the cloth sack directly in front of the spot where stood his heart, his soul: the girl he loved. He saw the rose and pink colored twizzles and knowing what was about to happen, he began to speak in rapid, pitter pat fashion.

"Hello and heavens above, Allura Rose! It's another fine day for collecting sweet forest flowers. How would you agree with me on that?" He had one eye on Allura Rose and one eye on the twizzles. "You look very beautiful today, if I may say so without being impolite. Oh...this is Bird...right here in my cloth carrying sack...I think you may have heard him chirping a bit earlier...he has a fine chirping voice. How would you agree with me on that? We rescued him a few days ago and he is improving very nicely...we found him in the forgetful flowers. We thought he was dead but as you can see, he's not.

The talking gold-colored fish back at our cave think he has a brother named Fred, but I really don't think so. But they think he is Fred's brother anyway. Isn't that silly?" Palryma was speaking so quickly that he did not notice Allura Rose pointing with near horror at the whirl of twizzles at his side.

"What is that!!" shrieked Allura Rose as she continued to point. That was all that Dalo needed to hear. The twizzles stopped and the young chalice maker's guide bowed at half-waist towards Allura Rose and made his famous introduction.

"I am Dalo," he said with a wry knowingness. "Dalo it is and Dalo you shall call me. Not Dallie, not Dalo-boy and certainly not Mr. Dalo. Just Dalo."

Palryma's shoulders slumped and he dropped his arms in resignation at his side. "Allura Rose, I would like you to meet my guide, Dalo. He has been with me since the day I was chosen. Actually, he volunteered to be my guide." he said in a more measured method of introduction. "I hasten to add that he is a very good guide. He just has this....well...sort of special way of introducing himself. There is no need for you to be alarmed. He's really a very friendly fellow......once you get to know him!"

Allura Rose stood there.....speechless, having dropped her hand basket of sweet forest flowers to the ground.

"I am pleased to make your acquaintance, Miss Allura Rose. I know that Pallie has been looking forward to kissing you!"

Palryma sunk to his knees in embarrassment and Bird tried to hide from sight in the cloth carrying sack by covering his tiny head with both wings.

"Of course" continued Dalo "the kissing will no doubt come later. Pallie needs more training first." Quickly realizing that his remark may be misinterpreted, Dalo was fast to add "Oh...I meant training in the ways of chalice making,

Miss Allura Rose....certainly not training in kissing! Oh no... Pallie assures me that he needs no training from me in the matters of kissing pretty girls! Do you Pallie!" Dalo looked over at Palryma who was now prostrate on his back with his hands covering his face and moaning something inaudible. The cloth carrying sack had slipped to Palryma's side and Bird was struggling not to be smothered by it.

Allura Rose noticed what neither Dalo nor Palryma did and she immediately knelt down to lift Bird from his struggle. "Come now Bird...you've only just been rescued by the "Kissing Master"....it would be unnatural for you to be squashed by him." she said with more than a touch of humor in her voice. She gently lifted Bird into the cradle of her arm and he began to chirp happily again. What she did not know was that he was chirping Palryma's favorite walking song "One Love for Me". What a lovely tune she thought to herself.

"You have a nice way with animals, Miss Allura Rose. It's the sign of a good heart. Pallie has a nice way with animals, too. He has some nice goats back home in Goosra....don't you Pallie!" Palryma had now rolled over on his stomach, covered his ears with his hands and muffled something into ground. "Dalo.....please stop...please."

"Oh come now Pallie...we are all friends here aren't we? Speaking of which, Miss Allura Rose....what do your friends call you? Are you always called Allura Rose? How about your family? What do they call you?"

"My friends call me Rose" she replied with ease and gentleness as she stroked Bird's feathers.

"Well lumpty-shoo-na, I think that's great, Rosie! I think we'll get along just fine. This will be fun...you and I and Pallie and Bird. Won't we have a great time of things, by rolly-toe! A great time!!"

The high morning turned into early afternoon which turned into late afternoon and the foursome did not notice how quickly the time was passing. They were becoming acquainted in a broad mix of childhood tales, laughter, jokes about Dalo's orange and black hair and the upcoming trip to the shore-by-the-sea. Rose's hand basket was now overflowing with every color of sweet forest flower they could find until she could barely manage to carry it. She wanted to make an especially beautiful bouquet with today's flower collection for her grandmother to commerate the meeting in the glen with Palryma and his two friends. Dalo enchanted Rose with stories of forest schwimmys and Bird continued to chirp "One Love for Me" because it was the only walking song he knew. They were both quite taken with Palryma's new love and from the looks of it, the feeling was quite mutual. After some initial misgivings, Rose had even become used to Dalo's calling her "Rosie". As for Palryma, even sunlight could not warm his young heart as much as his feelings for Allura Rose. "If being chosen as a chalice maker has brought me to her, I need no other explanation or reason for it." he mused as he relished in the sound of her laughter at Dalo's stories.

"I must be getting home now." said Rose "my grandmother will begin to wonder if the Shalatee Bears have eaten me up!"

"Yes...yes, I agree Rosie! You must not worry your grandmother and we must be getting back to our cave. We have a long journey to the shore-by-the-sea tomorrow. It's a big part of Pallie's training, you see."

"So you mentioned, Dalo." she replied as she began to place Bird back into the cloth carrying sack still slung around Palryma's broad shoulder.

As she did so, her head came as close to Palryma's as it had all day. Without warning, the young chalice maker planted the softest, sweetest kiss ever on her cheek. "I will bring you back something special from our trip to the shore-by-the-sea. Something very special." he whispered.

Rose did not blush nor did she pull away quickly. She placed Bird in the sack and lightly touched, with her hand, the spot on her cheek where she had just been kissed. "Thank you for a lovely day." she answered.

Witnessing all, as usual, Dalo remarked to himself "A quick learner who wastes no time! You clearly are the chosen one, young Palryma. Clearly the chosen one."

In parting, he shouted "We will see you again Rosie when we return from our trip to the shore-by-the-sea!! 'Till then, be well our new friend.....be well."

Night was closing in fast by the time Dalo, Bird and Palryma reached the cave. The Kura birds stopped their own singing by this time and by all accounts the gold-colored brook fish were retired for the night.

Dalo had a few quick bites of a sweet coulda and promptly went to bed. "Get some rest, Pallie, for we have much training to do tomorrow." was the last he spoke as he closed his eyes. Palryma fiddled a bit with the small chalice he had begun to work on only the day before. "I think I will make this one for Allura Rose. What do you say to that Bird?" Isn't that a good idea?"

Bird raised his head and knew it was time. "Sir..." he spoke with great hesitation. Palryma looked at him with amazement. "Bird?" he gasped, "was that you speaking!?"

"Yes Sir. It is I...Bird." he managed to barely get out "I have something I must tell you."

Chapter Thirteen

The morning sun's early rays of light blue and purple soaked the drapery of forgetful flowers that covered the cave. The brook had only begun to burble from a still water sleep that was uninterrupted by the jumping in and out of the water by the gold colored fish. The Kura birds collected themselves atop the opening of the cave but had yet to begin the day's musical symphony. Silent though they may have been for the moment, they were, as ever, observant and keenly aware that Palryma was sitting alone at the base of the cave in what clearly, to the Kura birds, was a state of despondency and troubled mind. It was not the character of the young chalice maker that they were used to witnessing. It created a point of concern for them as they felt the tenseness permeate the quiet of the morning air. They conferred briefly amongst themselves.

"Do you think he knows by now?" muttered one. "It surely seems as though he has heard something that worries him," muttered another.

"I think he has been told. Definitely has been told." said the highest singing Kura bird.

"I'll wager that Bird told him everything. The full whack! The look on his face says it all. I think he is stunned!"

"Better to have learned it directly from Bird than to find it out on his own." offered the oldest and wisest one. "I am sure that it took a good deal of courage for Bird to tell him the truth."

"Do you think he will quit the chalice making now?" said the youngest Kura bird as one of the gold colored fish stuck his head slightly above the water line. "Hi Pallie! It's early for you to be outside! The sun's rays are nice now aren't they? How was the kissing yesterday?"

"Go back underneath the water!" snapped Palryma. The startled fish disappeared in an instant and the Kura birds shook their heads as they began to hum a very quiet tune they thought might bring peace to the outside of the cave. Palryma looked as lost a man who had been wandering in the forest for years.

Inside the cave, Dalo awakened to the sight of Palryma's empty sleeping area. "He must be excited to get to the shore-by-the-sea to be getting such an early start." Dalo said with great yawn. "I'd best get my fat feet and wiggly toes moving or that young-and-in-love chalice maker will leave without me!" It was then that Dalo noticed Bird on the floor of the cave, limping his way towards the partially opened door. "And you too Bird! You are ready for such an early start?! I'm sure that Pallie will put you in the cloth carrying sack again today. You can't walk there on your own. Why, it'll take you forever! Probably longer than I was stuck next to those prattling will 'o the wisps in the wet fields! Ha!" Bird continued to limp towards the door.

"Sha-la-nee-sootee, Bird! Can't you hear me?" questioned Dalo. Bird turned to face him.

"I can hear you just fine Dalo." It was the first time Dalo had ever heard Bird speak.

"Sweet Lenora-ga! Do all the animals in this land speak? This is wonderful. You have a very nice speaking voice, Bird!" Bird turned away and continued towards the door.

Dalo turned but one flip in the air and landed directly in front of the exiting Bird. "What's going on here, by rolly-toe! Why are you walking away from me? Where is Pallie?"

"I fear I must go Dalo. I will miss you both very much. But I think my presence here is no longer wanted."

Dalo was confused and demanded an explanation. "Pallie is in training in this cave, Bird. If something is affecting that training I have a right to know what it is. He rescued you from near death and now you are leaving without an explanation. I am his guide! I insist you, at least, tell Pallie why you are going. He deserves an explanation!"

"I explained things to him last night after you fell asleep." was Bird's dejected reply.

"Well I am wide awake now, by rolly-toe!! I surely am wide-awake. Explain it to me!"

And so he did. Bird repeated the full story to Dalo who listened with careful concentration. When Bird finished, Dalo asked him where Palryma was. "I think he is outside."

"Wait here." commanded Dalo. "I will speak to him." Dalo marched, fat feet and wiggly toes and all, with determination outside to speak with his young chalice maker.

He found him sitting outside the cave and staring into and at nothing. He was rubbing one of the smooth stones his father gave him in-between his hands. "Pallie" said Dalo rather quietly "I've just had a talk with Bird."

"Then what do you want with me?" answered Palryma without looking at his guide.

"Well...I want to talk with you. I want to know why your reaction is so unlike you."

"Unlike me!?" said Palryma unbelievably "Unlike me? Is that what you say? If you knew me at all, you would not say such a thing!"

"Pallie.....Bird genuinely regrets what he did...he...."

The Chalice Maker interrupted him abruptly and shouted "Bad enough that Bird was a spy for that wretched King Hurrah III...bad enough that he fed him information about my comings and goings for years...but he tried to harm my parents, Dalo!!! He arranged with that sickly monarch to have the dark-as-night flying Reelatta Horses attack the home of my parents. I remember this vividly. My parents were shocked and my mother, especially, was terribly frightened. She worried for weeks that they might attack again! I remember this as though it was only yesterday. It took all the strength and faith of my father to restore her to calm. Even after they helped rebuild the damaged part of the house, no one in the whole village could understand why they attacked the home of my parents. Now I know. It was because of Bird...or shall I say the talking yellow bird Settela – the traitor!!

Dalo could not believe his ears. This was not his young chalice maker talking. Dalo knew he must do something quickly or all the training thus far would be for naught. It was his obligation as the guide. He had a duty...a promise to keep to Batoowa that he would train Palryma to be a chalice maker....and not stop one tiny step short of that goal.

"Pallie....Pallie, my friend....you are not thinking clearly at all. You must at least listen to me." Dalo pleaded. There was a palpable ache in the morning air and Dalo could feel it.

"Bird is trying to limp away from us forever, Pallie. Do you really want him to do that? After you rescued him and restored him to health? You saved him from certain death, Pallie. You fed him too-too-too berries and carried him in your cloth carrying sack. You taught him your favorite walking song so he could sing it at your wedding. I know this! He told me!"

"I never would have done any of those things had I known the truth about him!"

Dalo stepped back for a moment before he started to speak. "You have always known the truth about me, Pallie. You have always known what I did when I was a forest schwimmy. You've known from the beginning that I tried to steal the Cannerallo

Cupid flower from the wet fields and that I cursed Sweet Lenora-ga. You have always known all of that and still...if I can say so without being, as you like to say, impolite....you still like me. I think you still like me, Pallie......don't you?"

Palryma fixed a gaze from his violet eyes directly on his guide without smiling. "Of course, I like you Dalo. I like you for a lot of reasons. I like you because you told me all of that at the very beginning......the very beginning!

"But Pallie...listen to yourself...this is why I say you are not thinking clearly...Bird simply could NOT tell you anything in the beginning! He was near death and he certainly had no voice...even if he did, he certainly did not have the strength to speak. And, now you must admit this Pallie...surely you must admit that as soon as Bird found his voice...as soon as he knew he had the strength to speak...why, the first person he told the truth to was you!! And he did so without delay either. That must have taken some courage, Pallie – don't you think?

"I don't know what to think." Palryma shifted position to look more squarely at Dalo. "It's all so confusing, Dalo. Why must there be so much confusion?"

"Confusion exists so that we can figure things out, Pallie. That's all. We figure out the right things to do when we are confused and then we carry on."

"Well...how do I know what is the right thing to do? I am so angry with Bird, I don't know what to do."

"You can begin to sort things out by thinking clearly. Consider all of what I just told you. Bird was not deliberately trying to hide things from you...he simply could not tell you because he could not speak," explained Dalo "Anger is just like fear, Pallie. Do you remember what I told you about fear?"

Palryma nodded. "It's the same with anger" Dalo continued "it gets you nowhere and it allows you to do nothing good while you are in its grasp."

During their conversation, neither the chalice maker nor his guide noticed that Bird continued to make his way out of the cave and was limping towards the dirt path in a funerial manner. Finally, Dalo caught sight of him, tapped Palryma on his thigh and pointed at the sad sight of Bird walking away.

"It's up to you Chalice Maker....it's up to you." said the guide.

Palryma rose to his full height and took several long strides past the brook to where Bird was making his way. He scooped him up from the ground and held him in his strong hands. "Forgive me, Bird. I was rude in acting the way I did. Neither Dalo nor I want you to go away. I, especially, would like you to stay. I want you to be a part of my journey.....whatever it is. We'll have a great time, the three of us!!

"And Rosie, too?" asked Bird

Palryma laughed "Yes...and Rosie too!" He wiped away a tiny tear from Bird's tiny eye and Bird burst into song.

"Allright then....what are we waiting for?" shouted Dalo with glee. "We must go back inside and get ourselves ready for our trip to the shore-by-the-sea!! We're on another adventure!"

As the three friends made their way back inside the cave the Kura birds resumed their observations.

"The young chalice maker is now beginning to learn the ways, is he not?" said one.

"He is, indeed" said another. "He's a very quick learner, this young Palryma from Goosra. It will be interesting to observe him."

"It's a good thing he has a good guide." said the highest singer of the group.

Not the Kura birds, not Pallie nor Bird, as he rested on Palryma's shoulder — and certainly not Dalo noticed that another spot of orange hair on the back of Dalo's head had just turned black.

Chapter Fourteen

The three merry friends were well into their journey to the shore-by-the-sea when Palryma decided to finally ask his guide "Exactly how far is it, Dalo? We have been walking for hours. It seems to me that the forest is disappearing right before our eyes."

"Good question, Pallie. In fact, it's an excellent question. I wish I knew!"

"Dalo! You are always taking me to a place that you don't have any idea of its location!"

"But, Pallie my friend....don't I always get you there? Have faith. We must be nearing it or otherwise the trees of the forest would not be fading away."

It was at this point Bird offered some help. He had been resting on Palryma's shoulder since they left the cave, happy to be with them and happy that their reconciliation was complete.

"Sir...if I may" he peeped "I would agree with Dalo that I think we are quite near because the air has a salty scent to it, if you'll notice. That is a sure sign that not only are we headed in the right direction, but we are closer than you think."

"You see, Pallie!?" exclaimed Dalo "Bird agrees with me!" Palryma raised his hand and gave a quick stroke to Bird's plummed breast. "Maybe you are right, Bird. I do notice a different scent in the air now that you mention it. Have you ever been to the shore-by-the-sea?"

Bird paused a moment before his recollection and shifted his position slightly "Ah....yes, Sir. Only once before though and as a very young chirper. I barely had my full wing power when I followed my father one morning without his knowing. I thought he was headed out to gather some food for us but as it turned out he flew directly to the shore-by-the-sea first and gathered the food on his way back. It was further than I had ever flown before and when I realized that I was exhausted I couldn't turn back because I didn't know the route home!" Bird laughed at the silliness of his first big adventure "And when my father realized that I was following him, he took no mercy and said it served me right for not asking permission to come along in the first place." Bird laughed once again at the pluckiness of his own young self.

"What did you do?" asked Palryma with his own chuckle at the story's familiar ring of a young boy wanting too early to be a man.

"I flapped my new wings as though I would die any min-ute!!...but I kept pace with my father who looked like he was gliding all the way to the-shore-by-the-sea! When we finally got there I landed with a flop and could only gasp for air. It was then I remarked at how nice the salty air seemed to breathe. I was exhausted...but I made it!" Bird seemed very proud to be telling the story to his friends and he raised his beak a little bit in the air to show it.

"What a great story, Bird.....your father surely must have admired you for showing such great strength and determina-tion." said Palryma.

"Oh...I think he was proud of me for not giving up on the journey...but as I said, not too pleased that I tagged along without asking!"

"How did you make it back home to your family nest being as exhausted as you were?" Dalo wanted to know.

"My father carried me all the way home on his back as he flew." The recollection of that part of the story brought a glistening to Bird's eyes. No laughter. Just a glistening and a happy, reflective smile. All three were silent for a moment taken in as they were by the telling of Bird's fatherly tale.

Then Dalo spoke. "Maybe you'll feel like doing a bit of flying when we get to the shore-by-the-sea, Bird....you know... to remind you of happy days. Are you strong enough to fly?"

"I have been giving that some thought, now that you mention it, Dalo. I wouldn't mind giving it a try once we get there if the winds aren't too strong. If I remember correctly, there can be some heavy winds at the shore-by-the-sea."

"Only if you really feel like it, Bird." added Palryma cautiously "we can't have you back-tracking in your recovery!" Dalo nodded in agreement. "Do you want to sit in the cloth carrying sack till we arrive?"

"No thanks, Sir. I like being perched on your shoulder, as long as you don't mind it."

"You can perch there till the end of time, if you want Bird. Till the end of time." Palryma assured him. "It's no bother at all."

"I'm getting quite excited about getting there" Bird replied "and I have a better view of where we are going from up here on your shoulder. I'm certain that we are very near. The salt air is unmistakable."

"I have a great idea!" shouted Dalo "Let's all join in on one of Pallie's favorite walking songs. How about it, Pallie? Do you have any new ones for us? My big fat feet feel like thumping!"

Palryma feigned a scowl at his guide for the faint reference to the fact that all he ever whistled now since he met Allura Rose was "One Love for Me". "Do you feel up to learning a new one, Bird?" asked Palryma and Bird bobbed his head up and down and flapped his wings "I am ready, Sir!"

"This is one my father taught me after we finished hunting one day when I was a boy. It's named "We're Home at Last." Palryma whistled, Dalo thumped along and Bird chirped in harmony as the three made the final leg of their journey to the shore-by-the-sea.

While he whistled the new walking song Palryma thought to himself how blessed he was to have these two special friends. How very blessed.

It was not long before a crashing-like sound could be heard by all three as they climbed a long, steep hill towards what looked like to be a cliff in the distance. The more they climbed the hill, the clearer the sound became. Palryma picked up his walking pace and abruptly ended his whistling, as he was anxious to see what was making this strange sound. Bird kept breathing in deep breaths and whispered into Palryma's ear "I think we are here, Sir!" Dalo decided that, as guide, he should be the first one to the top of the hill and did 28 flips in the air and landed at the edge of the cliff in a whirl of blue and white twizzles. He sharply whipped around towards Palryma with his arms completely outstretched at his sides and shouted to the sky "It's the shore-by-the-sea, Pallie!! It's the shore-by-the-sea! We are here! We have made it!!" The wind was blowing his beard and hair in all different directions and it was plain to see that now there were very few strands of orange left in it. "Hurry Pallie! Come look for yourself! Wait until you see this! This is nothing like Goosra!"

Palryma began to dash up the last part of the hill's steep

incline as though he was born to run hills. Bird did a very delicate balancing act on his shoulders until Palryma came to a halt next to Dalo. He was astounded by what he saw. The shore-by-the-sea was massive. It stretched along for miles and the sea went out for what seemed like an endless blue horizon. High water, taller than two hunters, rose up and curled itself and then came falling down, only to disappear and be replaced by another row of high water, which did the very same thing. The repetition was never-ending. "What is that tall water doing over and over again with such force?" asked Palryma.

"Those are waves, Pallie! They are called sea waves." shouted Dalo.

"What a loud sound they make for water!" said Palryma

"They are crashing onto the shore-by-the-sea!" added Dalo

"When do they stop?"

"Hardly ever! That's their beauty...they only become a little bit smaller and then they start to crash all over again!"

Palryma shook his head in pure wonderment of it all. "Water that crashes to the ground with such a sound and then just disappears?! This truly must be a magical place!"

"You haven't seen anything yet, Pallie! Nothing!" exclaimed Dalo.

Palryma continued to shake his head in amazement. He took Bird off his shoulder and held him up in one hand. "What do you think of this Bird? Does it look familiar to you?"

"It's as beautiful as I remember it as a young chirper." Bird then began to flap his wings, first with a bit of energy and then with a frenzy. "Sir, I think I am going to fly!!" And with no more hesitation than that, Bird lifted himself off from Palryma's hand and took to flight for the first time since he was thrown out of the Castle of Hurrah III on that dark and fateful night. Dalo jumped up and down and clapped his hands and yelled "Yes! Yes! That is it Bird! Fly like you were meant to! Soar as high as you like!"

Palryma's violet eyes never once lost sight of Bird as he soared in circles above the sea waves. Bird rode the wind, glided effortlessly and flapped his way back in the direction of his two friends standing atop the cliff. "I am flying, Sir!! Can you see me!! Watch me fly!!" he shouted with glee as he swooped past them.

"We see you and we hear you, Bird!" acknowledged Palryma. "You look beautiful!"

Dalo tapped Palryma on the thigh and said "I think Bird is well now, Pallie. Don't you?"

"Yes. Yes I do. He seems to have made a full recovery." The chalice maker paused reflectively for a moment and continued "I hope he will not want to leave us now."

"Oh, Pallie....I wouldn't worry about that." replied Dalo in a more comforting tone "Bird is our friend now. He'll be our friend forever. Of this I am certain."

"I hope you are right, Dalo."

"I am as certain of it as I am that we must get ourselves off this cliff right now and down to the shore-by-the-sea. For there are things down there that I must show you! We can go down that narrow path over there. Follow me."

"I know one thing for certain Dalo" said the young chalice maker. "I know for certain that I will follow you anywhere!" And so he did. The guide and his young chalice maker made their way down to the shore-by-the-sea.

They had finally reached another destination and were about to add another part to their chalice making adventure.

Chapter Fifteen

Palryma's lungs were filled to the top with the refreshing and exhilarating sea air by the time he and Dalo reached the bottom of the hill. His sandy hair was already becoming dewy because of the mist from the waves carried by the gusts of wind blowing in from the restless sea. He felt like he was bursting with energy from the excitement of seeing the shore-by-the-sea for the first time. He kept one eye on the fascinating sea waves and the other on Bird who flew with an effortlessness that inspired Palryma. Dalo urged Palryma to remove his walking boots so that he could feel the white sand under his feet. "It's like nothing you will find in the forest, Pallie!" squealed Dalo. "Look how my toes are wiggling when they touch it."

Palryma was not so sure about walking barefooted on this new ground. He remembered all too well what happened to hunters in the wet fields when the wetness seeped right through their boots to trap them. He could only wonder what fate might await him if a similar sort of legend existed at the shore-by-the-sea. It was unfamiliar ground, to be sure, and the young chalice maker was cautious, to say the least. Dalo recognized his friend's hesitation.

"It's called sand, Pallie. It's like what you see on the dirt root paths of the forest but it's been completely dried out by the hot rays of the sun. It is so dry because the moisture in

it is all gone so it can only blow around all day. C'mon now....
take those heavy walking boots off!"

Palryma complied but with a very wary look on his face —
until he stood up again and set his bare feet in the sand. He
began to laugh and dance around at the same time.

"Isn't it great! Doesn't it feel wonderful on your feet?"
asked Dalo.

"This is just amazing! What a feeling! Why — there is
almost no need for walking boots at all!" exclaimed Palryma
as he began to dig his feet further into the sand. He started
to trot along the sand and immediately tripped over himself.
"It's not too good for running in though, is it Dalo?!"

Dalo brushed his beard aside, which was now blowing up
into his face and lifted his arm to point towards the sea. "If
you want to run, Pallie, you will have better luck racing right
along at the spot where the sea waves crash and disappear. The
sand over there is cooler and wet from the waves." Palryma
needed no further encouragement. He took off like a shot
for there was little else he liked better than to run as fast
he could. Dalo took heart in the youthful enthusiasm of his
trainee and sent a silent prayer up to Batoowa "You have done
more than just rescue me from the wet fields, Batoowa. You
have shown me what it is to be alive again. You have given me
Palryma and it is I who am learning from him. I am most
grateful, kind sir....most very grateful."

The reply was immediate. "Then it is time to show him
the treasures, is it not?"

"As you wish, sir. At your command." said Dalo "I am
merely the guide."

Just as Dalo set his gaze back on Palryma as he was speed-
ing down the shoreline, he saw him get tumbled by a sea wave.
Palryma fell flat on his stomach and immediately got covered
by another sea wave. Within a second, Dalo did seventeen flips

in the air and landed only a few feet from Palryma, whose hair and clothes were now soaked through. "Are you all right, Pallie?"

Palryma was laughing so hard that when he tried to get up and steady himself, he fell to his knees again and was knocked down from behind by yet another sea wave. He quickly moved closer to Dalo and out of the way of the sea waves. "This water tastes funny!" he said in between his pale of laughter. "And the sea waves seem like they want to grab my feet and take me away!" He shook his hair back and forth like a wet Simeeora boar and pushed it away from his face. "What an incredible place this is Dalo. We must return very soon and I will bring Allura Rose with me. She will not believe her eyes! You were right. This is nothing like the forest."

"Yes...perhaps we will return one day Pallie with your beloved but right now we must do what it is we came here for in the first place!"

"And what is that? You never said." Before Dalo could answer, Bird returned from his test flight and lowered himself onto Palryma's shoulder. "I think my wings are working just fine, Sir!" he said with pride. "Did you decide to go sea swimming?" All three laughed at Bird's innocent observation. "I think it was more at the invitation of the sea waves than my actual desire, Bird." replied Palryma.

"It's quite salty isn't it – the water I mean." said Bird.

"Ah.....yes!! That's it, Bird. Salt! I couldn't exactly figure it. That seems odd, doesn't it – salt in the water. The Shimmery Pond has no salt in it."

"The sea is full of it, Sir."

"How does it get there?" asked Palryma.

"I don't know, Sir.....I don't think my father ever told me."

Dalo did a flip in the air and shouted "You two must stop

talking right this minute or we will all be swept out to sea if we don't move away quickly. Look!!"

The sight they all saw was frightening. The water on the shore was returning to the sea with great speed and in the short distance appeared a sea wave the height of 20 hunters. The wind was changing into a very strong gust and the sand started to blow every which way. Palryma took Bird off his shoulder and held him close to his chest. "What do we do, Dalo? Where shall we go?'

"Run, Pallie! Run up to that high hill of sand with the green shoots coming out of it. Run and hide behind it or we will surely be swallowed up by this mountainous sea wave!" Palryma turned away from the sea quickly. He held Bird closely with one arm and scooped Dalo up by his waist with the other and began to run for dear life. "Let go of me, Pallie! Put me down! What are you doing?"

"I am saving you!" said Palryma as he ran directly against the strong head winds.

"I can do my flips over to the sand hill!" protested Dalo.

"Not in this wind, you can't! Within one flip, the wind will carry you out to meet that wall of water heading straight our way.....now stop wiggling!!" In no time the strength and speed of the young chalice maker brought he and his friends to safety behind the sand hill. They all peered just above the top of it to watch the events unfolding at sea. The mountain of water headed towards the shoreline got closer and closer.

"Sweet Lenora-ga...have you ever seen anything like this?" said Palryma "Are we all going to perish here at the shore-by-the-sea?"

Then it all dawned on Dalo. Batoowa was about to reveal some of the treasures he spoke about. "I think we will be all right, Pallie. No need to worry."

"What! No need to worry? Are you completely crickeycrackey?"

Dalo smiled. "Why, Pallie! You are speaking the silly language! That's wonderful."

"There's nothing wonderful about being swallowed up by salty water!! We have to run further away."

"No, I think not." said Dalo thoughtfully "We will be protected. We must watch and see what happens now."

As Dalo spoke, Bird managed to lift his head up from Palryma's protective hand and look up to the sky. "Sir" he said, "look at all those fellow flyers near the wall of water. They are gathering. I can tell from the way they fly in motion. There must be something behind that sea wave. Something that is of great interest to all those birds."

Dalo, Palryma and Bird all watched and were stunned by what was happening. No one moved. No one could.

The giant sea wave completely disappeared just as it looked as though it might crash down upon the shore-by-the-sea with the force of a thousand gods. The sea seemed completely still for a moment until there appeared, where the mountain of water had been only a few moments before, a sight only few in the land had ever seen.

It was a fish bigger than the size of one hundred Castles of Hurrah III all put together. It's skin was bluer than any sky with eyes larger than the whole of the Shimmery Pond. It lifted itself halfway out of the water to reveal a mouth so wide that it could swallow an entire village. It dove back into the water and its dive showed a tail so big that entire families of Shatoo birds could rest on it. Palryma looked up and down the sea coast and wondered where he could run with his friends for further protection. "Stay still, Pallie." commanded Dalo.

"We cannot stay here Dalo! What if this water creature has legs and begins to walk out of the sea towards us?"

"It does not have legs. I know now what this is, Pallie. It is called a whale. It is from far, far out into the sea."

"A whale? What kind of fish is this whale? Is it for eating? What is it doing so close to the shore-by-the-sea?"

"Well...it's definitely not for eating, Pallie."

The whale lifted itself again halfway out of the water and seemed as though it was looking straight at Palryma. "Sweet Lenora-ga, Dalo...we have been spotted by this whale! He looks straight at us!"

"Yes...I can see that he does. I think he is friendly, by rolly-toe! I think this is a friendly whale. I will go to greet him right now." As soon as the words came out of his mouth, Dalo did 21 flips in the air and landed just at the spot where the dry sand met the wet sand. "No!! No, Dalo...come back here." screamed Palryma. It was too late. Dalo was already there.

"Hello and heavens above, Whale!" You are one fine big fish, are you not? How would you agree with me on that?" Palryma was running with Bird as fast as he could towards Dalo and waving his free arm wildly. "Stop, Dalo. Stop!" Dalo turned towards Palryma with a quizzacle look on his face. "Stop shouting like you are some crickey-cracky man, Pallie! I am just trying to talk to this friendly whale."

"You have not been introduced, Dalo. It is impolite to speak unless you are introduced. I have told you that before!"

"What!! Even to whales?"

"Everyone, Dalo. Including whales."

"Oh alright...have it your way." Bird was watching all that transpired and wondered if he was the only one who noticed that the whale was getting much closer than before.

Dalo shouted at the top of his lungs "Hello, Whale! I am Dalo. Dalo it is and Dalo you shall call me. Not Dallie, not Dalo-boy and certainly not Mr. Dalo!" The guide smiled broadly and his toes began to wiggle on his fat feet. "How was that, Pallie? Good enough?"

"I guess that will have to do. We should wait for an answer, though." The whale's answer was not long in coming and when it arrived, it arrived in a huge shower of water from a hole in the top of the whale's head all over Palryma, Dalo and Bird. When he was done, the whale disappeared again under the sea.

"That is a very strange response." said Palryma wiping his face "I don't know if that is polite or impolite as I have never met a whale until just today."

"Look Sir!" said Bird "I think the whale rises again!"

And indeed Bird was correct. The whale rose just enough to let the three friends see the huge hole at the top of his head. "Oh, by rolly-toe I think we are going to get showered with water again! Maybe we should move back a bit!" cried Dalo. And so they did. But it was to no avail at all for the shower from the whale this time was not water. No indeed. It was definitely not water.

Instead, hundreds and hundreds and hundreds of tiny round and white objects flew high out of the hole in the top of the whale and came raining down upon them as they tried to quickly back away from the sea.

"Ow!" said Palryma as he was pelted with them. "What are these things! They are hard like stones."

"By rolly-toe! These are little pearls, Pallie. These are jewels of the sea! These are some of the treasures Batoowa spoke about! They are for you! They are for you to take back to the cave and use to make your chalices! I told you this was a friendly whale!"

The raining down of the little pearls ended when the last one hit the sand. Palryma looked around and there were hundreds of them lying on the sand, up and down the shore, glistening in the sun. It was a brightness the likes of which he had never seen. He picked one up to examine it more closely. "They are quite beautiful, aren't they Dalo? They are perfectly round in shape and are so shiny that they almost glimmer. I think you are right...they could look very pretty adorning my new chalices." He looked straight out to sea and screamed "Thank you, Whale! Thank you for helping me make my new chalices." The whale rose up again and turned on its side only to dive deep back into the sea. His big tail was to last to submerge and it seemed to wave good-bye or maybe good luck to Palryma as the whale disappeared entirely from sight.

"Whatever will we do with all these shiny little pearls, Dalo? Should we take them all back to our cave?"

"I think we should remember the Legend of Replacements right now, Pallie. Take only as many as you think you will need. We can come back again if need be. Remember, if you only take what you need, there will always be enough. The ones we don't carry back will be washed back into the sea by the sea waves. Back to where they came from. As it should be."

Dalo and Palryma began to pick some of the tiny pearls out of the sand and put them in the cloth carry sack. "I don't think Bird will mind." said Palryma "I think he would rather fly now than have me carry him in the sack."

"Probably true, Pallie. Probably true." replied Dalo as he brushed the sand off some of the pearls he picked up. "Where is Bird, anyway? He was just here. Has he flown off again to test his wings?" Palryma shrugged his shoulders. No sooner than the shrugging of his shoulders had finished did Bird appear in the sky overhead. "Sir!" he shouted from high above "Sir, I must tell you what I have seen in my flying!"

"Come down here Bird and tell us properly...we can't hear everything you say from way up there!" jested Palryma. "Even my big long ears can hardly hear you, Bird" added Dalo "Come down and tell us what excites you so!" Bird seemed to nose dive from the sky in his hurry to land on Palryma's shoulder. "Lumpty-shoo-na, Bird! You must be more careful how you dive out of the sky. You have only just begun to fly again!" warned Dalo.

"Oh, Sir!" exclaimed Bird "I must tell you what I have seen! Never before, Sir, have I seen such a sight. Not even the whale and tiny pearls can compare!"

"Bird! Calm down!" said Palryma "You are practically breathless! Just tell us what you have seen. Are we in danger?"

"No Sir" answered Bird in between gulps of breath "I do not think we are in danger....I mean I can't really say for sure. I don't know what power they hold."

"What power are you talking about...who holds what power?" asked Dalo with a stern look on his face. "Is someone nearing us?"

"Not *who*, Dalo" replied Bird "*It*...I mean them!"

"Bird...now take a breath and calmly tell us what you mean." instructed Palryma.

"The trees, Sir! The shiny trees and shiny bushes! They nearly blind your eyes!"

"Where are these trees, Bird?" said Dalo

"Over beyond the sand hill where we were hiding from the whale. There is a gully just beyond it and in the gulley I saw these shiny trees and bushes. I nearly fell out of the sky they blinded me so!"

"Sit on my shoulder here, Bird, and point us towards the way." said Palryma. "We will see about these trees and bushes."

And off they went.....the three of them to look at the shiny trees at the shore-by-the-sea.

Chapter Sixteen

The gulley was, indeed, not far away – just as Bird had described. The afternoon clouds had already begun to roll in from the sea and provided a cover overhead from what might have otherwise been a blinding shininess that could be seen on an approach to the gulley. Still, even with the cloud covering there was a strange glow emanating from the gulley that indicated to all who came near that, perhaps, something out of the ordinary was down there. Dalo was in the lead as the trio carefully tread closer with every step to the edge of the gulley. Bird decided to stay perched on Palryma's shoulder for this trip and kept signaling for Dalo to keep walking straight ahead. The ever-adventuresome chalice maker made his approach somewhat cautiously – a bit uncharacteristic for the fearless 23-year old, but he was protecting the large collection of tiny pearls resting in the cloth carrying sack. He wanted to make certain that whatever he encountered in the gulley would not attempt to make off with his jewels of the sea. He had many plans on how to use them as adornments for the new chalices – especially the one he intended on creating for his new love, Allura Rose.

"And then there are the ones I have already started making for my parents" he thought silently to himself as he continued to walk towards the gulley "these tiny pearls will look beautiful on those and I think I will also make a nice one for Dalo — just to show him how much I appreciate all he has done for me as my guide. And, of course, there's Bird — I think I will make him a very special one that has a very low stem and wide cup so he can drink out of it — perhaps even bathe!" Palryma's musings were cut short by an unforgettable exclamation from Dalo as he stopped short at the top of the gulley and looked down upon the magical sight below.

"Sweet Lenora-ga, we are in the land of the chalice maker now!!!"

"What do you see, Dalo?" Is it safe to go down there?' asked Palryma as he hurried to catch up to his guide.

"Batoowa" prayed Dalo "you have led us to this gulley of wonderment and I ask only now that you deliver my chalice maker safely back to his cave."

Batoowa replied immediately — but only Dalo could hear him. "It was you Dalo, who guided young Palryma to the shore-by-the-sea. I only put the shiny trees and bushes here for him. You are a good guide, Dalo. You have done as we asked. You have helped bring our chosen one a long way from his hunter background in Goosra. We are very pleased with you."

"I do not ask for myself, Batoowa — only for Palryma. These treasures will attract a foreign and wicked heart. Safe journey back to the cave is all I ask."

There was no further reply from Batoowa.

Palryma took his last few strides and was soon standing next to Dalo looking down into the gulley. Bird began to excitedly flap his wings. "You see for yourself now Sir!" he exclaimed, "look how shiny the trees and bushes are!"

"What hangs from the branches of those trees, Dalo? I have never seen anything like it. Is it some kind of shiny fruit?"

"They are not pig-nittys from the forest! And they are definitely not for eating!" replied Dalo. "Follow me, Pallie!" Dalo began his short descent into the shallow gulley to begin to walk among the shiny trees. "Have a care not to spill any of your tiny pearls on the way down." he added. Palryma followed, squinting his eyes the closer he got to the gulley floor. Soon all three were standing right next to one of the trees.

"What are these things?" asked Palryma again, reaching his hand up to touch the object. "They are quite beautiful and all lovely different shapes. I have never, ever seen a color green so brilliant and clear."

"They are called emeralds, Pallie!" said Dalo "All emeralds are green and shine so brilliantly."

"And they are known to grow on trees like this?" inquired Palryma, with some doubt in his voice.

"Well....I'm not too sure about everywhere, Pallie, but they certainly do grow on trees at this shore-by-the-sea!" answered Dalo.

"They are quite pretty, indeed, Sir" added Bird "What are they called again, Dalo?....emmeras, did you say?"

"Em-er-alds" answered Dalo "Em-er-alds" he repeated, adding emphasis on each syllable.

"I have never seen anything like them anywhere in the land" announced Bird.

Palryma began to pick the emeralds off the trees as if they were sweet forest flowers. He took all sorts of different shapes and sizes and placed them alongside the tiny pearls in his cloth carrying sack. "Em-er-alds" he whispered aloud, repeating Dalo's emphasis. "What a glorious thing they are. Harder than stones yet they grow on trees. Allura Rose will hardly believe this story when I tell her."

"And Sir, don't forget the other shiny things on those bushes at the end of this row of emerald trees." said Bird pointing with his wing. Palryma could see that Dalo was already inspecting the row of bushes Bird referred to. They were much smaller than the trees and not bearing green colored things at all. "And what is the name of that thing you now hold in your hand, Dalo?"

Dalo turned his head towards Palryma and raised his hand to show what he was holding.

"These shiny red things are called rubies, Pallie! Red and shiny and more round than the emeralds....but still very pretty in their own right, don't you think?" Palryma agreed. "Their color is very deep and soft. It is almost royal, it seems, to look at it. How would you agree with me on that, Dalo?"

"It surely has a majestic quality about it, no doubt, Pallie. I think I like them better than the emeralds. You should definitely put some into your cloth carrying sack. Your chalices would look very nice with a few rubies in them!"

"I like these round red rubies" said Palryma as he picked a number of them and carefully placed them into his cloth carrying sack next to the emeralds and tiny pearls. Dalo could see that the afternoon sky would soon give way to evening dusk and they would not be able to make their way back to the cave before the full dark of night arrived. "I think we should sleep under the stars tonight, Pallie. We have had a long day and with a good night's rest we will be better able to make the walk from the shore-by-the-sea back to our cave in good time. How would you agree with me on that?"

"I would agree with you in every way possible, Dalo....for I am a bit tired from a long day's journey and feel flushed from the salt air. A restful night will do us well, don't you think so, Bird?"

"Whatever pleases you, Sir. I have never been one much for flying at night anyway." was the reply.

As Dalo, Palryma and Bird strolled their way out of the shallow gulley, the sun made a hasty retreat below the horizon. Dalo suggested that they rest for the night at the high sandy hill with green shoots coming out of it. They would be protected there from the sea winds and could lie in comfort. Palryma remarked on how quickly the sun disappeared from the sky at the shore-by-the-sea. "It's as though the moon and the sun fight for a space in the sky. It is quite a magical place this shore-by-the-sea, Dalo. Thank you again for bringing me here." he said as he made a comfortable place for himself to lie against the sand hill.

"It's all part of the training, Pallie! All part of the training."

"You know, Dalo...with the light from this high moon on your head, it looks like there is not a single strand of orange hair left on it."

"Oh yes! I believe it is all gone. I won't miss it that's for sure. Black is my natural color as I have told you!" said Dalo with a smile.

"You are a good guide, Dalo," said Palryma earnestly. "The very best."

"It's what I wanted to be, Pallie" replied Dalo softly. "You rest your head now. I want to walk over to the sea and stick my fat feet and wiggly toes in it. They need a good cooling off, by rolly-toe!" Palryma easily closed his eyes and Dalo turned to walk to the sea.

As Palryma noted, the moon was, indeed, very high in the sky — almost lighting the way for Dalo to get to the shoreline as he tried in vain to whistle one of Palryma's walking songs. "I guess I'll never get that whistling part correct." he mused,

"I wonder how Pallie does it."

Dalo's pre-occupation with whistling was too strong and the moon was too high and he failed to notice the stealth-like swooping of two dark-as-night flying Reelatta horses who moved silently down from the sky. They landed without a sound on either side of Dalo as he let the sea wash over his fat feet and wiggly toes. When he looked up both horses were reared up on their hind legs ready to strike. Dalo tried to run but his fat feet were not made for running and four hooves came crashing down on his head. The victorious whinny of the horses alerted Bird who was still awake. He immediately took to flight towards the sound. He flapped his wings as fast as he could but he could see Dalo's still body lying in between the horses.

"I know you horses!!" screamed Bird as he flew like a bullet towards them. "I know who you are and I know where you came from! Get away from my friend!!" The horses whinny grew louder into a whipping war cry and awakened Palryma. He could only see the horses at the shoreline. He could not see Dalo. He heard Bird scream again "Get away from my friend!"

As he got closer to one of the horses, Bird flew straight up into the sky around to the other side of his enemy from the Castle of Hurrah III. Like a diving arrow, he descended like lightning and plunged his beak deep into the horse's eye drawing a spurting blood that gushed onto the sand. Bird withdrew immediately and flew up into the night again. Repeating his attack, this time he flew around to the stunned equine's other eye and nearly plucked it out with the force of his plunge.

"Get out...get out...get away from here!" he screamed and screamed again. The horses winged their way up from the shore and made haste away. The blinded horse knew no direction and flew out to the sea and disappeared deep into it. The other flew away.

Palryma dashed with all his might to Dalo's side and knelt beside him as he raised him up into his arms.

"Dalo!!! Dalo!! Talk to me!!" he pleaded. "Say something!"

Dalo turned his head ever so slightly "The moon's light was too bright, Pallie. I was not paying attention and I guess they saw me. I am so sorry to be leaving you, my friend."

NO!!! No, Dalo...please...don't you leave me!! Please!! I still need you." begged Palryma.

Dalo moved his head from side to side. "It is time, Pallie."

"No...no..no Dalo! It is not time. You can't leave...I don't know all the ways yet."

Dalo's breathing was becoming more and more shallow.

"I will get them Dalo. I will get these horses and whoever sent them to harm you. I swear I will. I will not rest until they are dead. I will get your revenge!"

Dalo summoned whatever strength was left in his battered little body. "No, Pallie. Promise me you will not seek revenge. It does no good."

Palryma could hardly hear his guide for the choking back of his own tears.

"Please, Pallie...promise me this before I die. No revenge. It is not right for a chalice maker to seek revenge. You must understand this."

"I understand nothing," cried Palryma through his streaming tears "Please do not leave me...please....I will be lost without you."

"Promise me..." whispered Dalo.

"Alright, Dalo....I promise you I will not seek revenge. I will promise you anything, but please stay."

"Alright then. Freh-nit high, Pallie. Do you remember when I taught you that when we first met? "You remember don't you? It means 'I'll see you soon!'" You must remember that."

"I will try to remember all that you taught me" he sobbed. Palryma drew Dalo closer to him and heard the last whisper of life's breath leave his guide's body. The chalice maker screamed up into the night sky "NO!! No...please...please make this not so."

But it was so. Dalo was gone. In complete despair, Palryma could only set Dalo's lifeless body gently onto the sand and covered his tear soaked face in his trembling hands.

"Freh-nit high, my friend. Freh-nit high, my guide. I will never forget you."

Bird limped closer to Dalo and Palryma. "I tried to help, Sir. I tried to help but I was too late. I am very sorry."

The young chalice maker did not hear him. For he had already begun to weep like he had never wept before. He wept and wept and wept. He wept until the sun came up and when he thought he could weep no more, he continued to weep.

It was as though Palryma would weep forever.

End of Part One

Part Two

Chapter Seventeen

The quiet roll of early morning waves at the shore-by-the-sea advanced only so far as to mark an invisible fence at Palryma's legs through which, it seemed, only the violet rays of the sun were permitted to pass through. Their color was the only reminder that the young chalice maker, indeed, had violet eyes but were now red and sore from the inconsolable weeping with which he mourned the loss of his beloved guide. Palryma's face was more forlorn than a young man's should ever be and his heart was heavier than a man who had to watch one of his own children suffer and die. It was a night of paralytic grief. The day's promise lay unattended and over-shadowed by this unparalleled funeral remorse. Bird stayed huddled in the tiny space between the lifeless body of Dalo and the limp frame of Palryma. He had heard no sound emi-nate from Palryma's mouth save for a keening woe for hours and hours. The haunting state of play began to worry him and he finally spoke.

"Sir" he whispered "is there anything I can do to ease your pain? Anything at all? You've only to ask."

Palryma responded without a sound....without parting

his lips. He looked down at Bird with a vacuous stare and stroked his bloodied wing feathers, only once, with a gentle almost protective touch. "What shall we do, Sir?" asked Bird "Whatever shall we do now?"

The chalice maker began to rise very slowly. First to a full kneeling position where he squinted out to sea and never letting go of Dalo's hand. He looked inward and then back out to sea. His sand-caked and sea-soaked hair lay matted against his head framing an awkward reminder of the night. He continued to rise to his full height and in a timid and cautious swoop lifted Dalo from his temporary resting place to the solace of his hunter's chest. He used his free hand to move Bird from his sentinel spot in the sand to the turret lookout point on his sturdy shoulder. He began a silent procession, cradling Dalo all the way, back to the high sandy hill with green shoots coming out of it. It was the place where the three travelers spoke their last words to each other. The previous afternoon had left them merry with excitement about the treasures of the shore-by-the-sea. The morning's light found their lives inextricably changed forever. Palryma could not speak. He could think of nothing to say.

Moving behind the high hill of sand and protected against the rising wind, Palryma laid Dalo down carefully positioning his arms on his chest and resting in his long beard....his long, totally black beard. He reached up and took Bird off his shoulder placing him in the cup of his two hands.

"You have to do something for me, Bird. It's very important."

Relieved just to hear the sound of Palryma's voice again, Bird responded "Sir. I will do anything. Just name it."

"I must ask you to fly home....not to our cave, but to my home in Goosra. Surely you know the way." Bird nodded.

"You must tell my father that I am coming home. Tell him that I am coming home to bury my guide. Tell him that I want to bury Dalo along the edge of the Shimmery Pond, amongst the Surrupta trees. Ask him to call upon Swee-Hara, the forest cleaner to help him clear a spot. He will understand."

"Sir, I do not think your parents know who I am." Palryma told him not to worry about that. "Simply tell them that you are my friend. They will ask for no more introduction than that."

"Is that all you want me to do. Just deliver that message."

Palryma shook his head. "No. Ask my father to direct you to the homes of my childhood friends, Siglatee and Moralna. Gather them both together and give them the directions to our cave. Tell no one else except Siglatee and Moralna and impress upon them that they are to tell absolutely no one where our cave lies. Tell them that I want them to build a litter so that we can carry Dalo into Goosra. They know how to build one. Remind them of the time we built one for the cousin of Simmee-Sammy, the village historian when we were young boys and the cousin broke his leg chasing after a forest schwimmy. Remind them that it is in the Book of Events. They will know exactly what I mean. Go along with them from Goosra to the cave to see that they take no wrong turns, but they must never tell anyone where the cave is. I will be waiting for you inside the cave when you arrive."

"But, Sir how will you, yourself, get back to the cave from the shore-by-the-sea? How will you take Dalo back all by yourself?'

Palryma looked again at the body of his guide resting lifelessly in the sand. Before the crippling sadness could overcome him once more, he responded "I will carry Dalo on my back. Just as your father did for you when you were too tired to fly back home from your first trip to the shore-by-the-sea. I will leave immediately as should you. It's still early morning and I think you should be well able to fly to Goosra before the sun sets today. If I move steadily along, I can be back at our cave by nightfall. But we have no time to lose."

Bird seemed unsure of what to do. He did not want to leave Palryma alone to make the journey back to the cave. The chalice maker could sense Bird's hesitation. "Bird" he said with quiet authority "it is very important that you do this for me. We must make arrangements to bring Dalo back to Goosra. I need your help." That was all that Bird really needed to hear.

"I will leave immediately, Sir, but please be careful on the way back."

"I will be fine, Bird. I have Dalo with me." With that, Bird flapped his wings and headed for the skies of Goosra with the determination of a kingly bird on a royal mission.

Palryma looked around him at the endless roll of the waves and the ever shifting sand at the shore-by-the-sea and wondered if he would ever return — knowing full well that if he ever did, it would be without his trusted guide. He noted that everything at the shore-by-the-sea seemed blissfully unaffected by the transpired events of the night. "It's as though the waves continue to crash and disappear as if everything was the same. Maybe being here just once was enough." he said as he strapped Dalo to his back with the sea-weed rope that lay everywhere. "Maybe I don't ever have to see this shore-by-the-sea again. It has taken much away from me." Cinching Dalo's body properly in a balanced place on his muscled back, Palryma reached down to grab his cloth carrying sack full of tiny pearls, shiny green emeralds and deep red rubies. As he slung the jewel filled sack carefully across his chest he looked at them with resignation. "These treasures have cost me dearly. I might just as soon lived without any of them." With the careful placement of one foot surely in front of the other, the chalice maker made straight away for the forest outside of Goosra from whence he came. His sharp eyes plotted the route back home to the cave. Never once looking back at the shore-by-the-sea.

Just after the sun passed a noon day spot high in the sky, Palryma came upon a fork in the dirt path that he did not recall seeing on the original journey to the shore-by-the-sea. He scolded himself for not paying closer attention to Dalo on the way. "I spend too much time whistling walking songs when I should be paying attention to where I am going." He looked around for any familiar forest signpost that would indicate which fork he should follow. He saw none but knew, even though he was confused, he must make a decision. It was imperative that he reach the cave before dark. "I think there was a Loo-Hoo-Hoo tree somewhere down here in the dis- tance." he said as he peered rather bemusingly towards his left. "I wish I could be certain of it, though. I don't mind being confused, but I hate to be lost."

He was about to move along the left fork when he heard the most appealing chirping of two Willa-Whattie birds, the tiniest birds in the forest. Two of them could literally sit on a grown person's thumb and not obscure the thumbnail. They always traveled in twos and when they chirped, they sounded like an entire village singing the legend songs of Sweet Lenora-ga. Palryma turned to his right to see if he might catch sight of the tiny birds. Because of their size, it was, nat- urally, not an easy thing to do. Spotting a Willa-Whattie bird was nigh on to spotting a forest schwimmy – but not quite.

Palryma was not surprised when he did not see the birds, but he was truly and almightily shocked at what he did see – a row of Cannerallo Cupid flowers had appeared from nowhere lining both sides of the right fork in the dirt path — unmistakable for their distinctive orange and black petals. For the first time since the awful events at the shore-by-the-sea, the young chalice maker smiled. It was a wry smile nonetheless because he sensed that his deceased guide was still watching over him. He reached back with his right hand and gave a loving touch on the top of Dalo's head. "I knew you would not forsake me, my friend." Palryma took a deep breath of the crisp forest air and was determined to do what he had set in his mind to do earlier that day at the shore-by-the-sea. "Take me home, Dalo!" he said with raised arms "You will forever be my guide!" More determined now than before to make it back to the cave before dark, Palryma increased his stride and almost without thinking began to whistle one of his walking songs. Dalo's body was still securely strapped to the young chalice maker's back and clearly, it seemed, guiding him back home. The only thing missing was the thumping along of Dalo's fat feet and wiggly toes. With each step forward Palryma moved closer to home. As he rounded the bend he could not see behind him that the Cannerallo Cupid flowers had now disappeared just as quickly as they appeared.... back to the wet fields from whence they came.

Palryma kept a steady pace through the forest and walking on he was reminded of how comfortable and natural he felt amongst the tall trees and ground covering plants of every kind. The forest smelled sweet to him. Its intoxicating allure held sway over him since he was a young boy hunting and foraging through it all with his father. The acrid taste of salt in the air that permeated the shore-by-the-sea was not one that appealed to Palryma's keen senses. He knew that his real treasures, the ones that mattered to him most in life, lie not in gulleys of emeralds and rubies but here among the sweet forest flowers. It was the forest that brought him to life. It was the shore-by-the-sea that brought death to him. "I might go back one day" he mused "but only to show Allura Rose what an unusual place it is. I am in no hurry to return." He thought more and more about his love, Allura Rose, the closer he got to the cave. He wondered aloud about having Bird fly to meet her and explain Palryma's extended absence. He then thought for a moment that he should bring her to the burial of Dalo by the Shimmery Pond. "They got along so well and Dalo really was very fond of her." But then he thought again that a burial setting was not the most appropriate nor cheery setting for Allura Rose to meet his parents for the first time. "No, their first meeting should be a happy time – one that all can look back on with joy and celebration. I will arrange for a proper meeting after I have taken care of Dalo – after I have comfortably rested his bones for good aside the Shimmery Pond."

Whistling and walking....walking and whistling.....time passed and the sun moved lower in the sky. Its blue had not yet started to mix with the creeping, darker shadows that always brought in the night but Palryma knew that time was nearing. He refused to admit that he was growing weary and longed to sit for awhile at the babbling brook outside the cave and have a cool bowl of water. "What I wouldn't give for a sweet coulda right now" he sighed "but I must keep moving on. There will be enough to eat and drink when I get to the cave. I'm sure I must be near."

He was right. Palryma could see in the field at the bottom of the hill, a growing patch of forgetful flowers. That was a sure sign that the path leading to the cave was not far off. "We're almost there, Dalo. Almost home." Palryma's pace quickened 'till he was walking through the spreading fields of forgetful flowers. Down one hill and up another and then he stopped. It was not more than 300 yards in the distance. The unassuming cove where lie the babbling brook and the cave covered in forgetful flowers. The place from which he and Dalo and Bird left with so much adventure and promise was now silently beckoning the chalice maker's return with the body of his dead guide tied to his back. Palryma's legs almost went weak with the notion that Dalo's laughter would never fill the cave ever again. There would be no more adventures or trips and no more instructions from the little man with orange and black hair.

All Palryma's time with Dalo at the cave was now history and, strangely, what he remembered on this long approach to the cave was Dalo's last instruction to him: "Do not seek revenge. It is not fitting for a chalice maker to seek revenge."

Chapter Eighteen

Palryma walked right past the cool waters of the babbling brook and reached under the drooping veil of forgetful flowers to push on the spot in the rock that opened up the heavy stone door to the cave. He did not acknowledge, or even notice, that the Kura birds were sitting in their usual spot atop the cave. He did not notice that even though night had not yet officially arrived over the land, the birds were not singing. Had he looked up at all, he would surely have noticed that the Kura birds were grave and sullen — so unlike them. He did not see that the gold colored fish in the brook did not jump out to happily greet him, as was their habit. He did not see that the three fish were gathered in the corner of the brook with their heads just barely tipped above the water line — just enough so that could watch Palryma's return in silence. If Palryma had noticed any of these things, he might have learned that the Kura birds and the gold colored fish in the brook had been expecting him. They knew he would be returning with Dalo's body strapped to his back. News like that did not stay secret in the land for long. They were watching out for him and waiting...and were silent for a reason.

Once inside the cave, Palryma moved directly towards Dalo's sleeping area and laid him to rest on that comfy spot that his guide loved so well. He turned to take a seat at the work table and began to wonder how it was that their shore-by-the-sea adventure had gone so awry without warning. How could it be that the little man who so enthusiastically led them on that adventure now lay dead in the chalice maker's cave? Death was a new phenomenon to Palryma. He had not experienced much of it in his short life. He remembered when his father's father, Wilyatam, died. Palryma was but 10 years old at the time and did not think more of it than now he would have to go into the forest alone to collect sweet forest flowers and pig-nittys. Beforehand, it was always the special trip he made with his grandfather, hand in hand. So, at that time he did not grieve as the adults in the village did. He remembered that Simmee-Sammy, the village historian was besotted with tears as he recorded the burial day of Wilyatam, father of Bestra in the Book of Events.

This time death was different. This time Palryma's heart was breaking. He now saw death through the eyes of a young man, not a young boy, and he was therefore connected to real grief. His only solace was in knowing that as soon as Siglatee and Moralna arrived with the litter to carry Dalo, Palryma would be on his way back to Goosra — returning home to see his beloved parents. "I have missed them so." he said aloud as he picked up the smooth stones his father gave to him when he departed Goosra. "I need to talk to my father." He wanted desperately to tell Bestra about some of the things he had learned from Dalo. He wanted to tell him all about the shore-by-the-sea. Above all, he wanted to tell him about Allura Rose.

For no other reason than he thought he should, Palryma took a blanket from the wall shelf and laid it on Dalo as though to comfort him while he slept. He did not cover his face as the finality of that act would make it seem as though

Dalo had disappeared. Palryma was not ready for that just yet. He wanted to pretend that Dalo could watch him as he began to make the burial marker out of the blue and pink spotted rock they had collected together. "It's not going to be a chalice, my friend" he said to the body in the corner "but I will use the gifts you taught me and make a marker that all the village of Goosra will be proud to see."

Palryma began to work through the night. He did not know when Siglatee and Moralna would arrive at the cave with Dalo's litter and he wanted to be ready. He used his molten hands to scoop out of what was left of the blue and pink spotted rock, a piece that was large enough and well suited for a burial marker. He plied away with his fingers and carefully chipped away with his special tools. He fashioned a three cornered stone that would lie just high enough above the ground at the Shimmery Pond to be seen from the back window of his parent's home. It was rough hewn on the sides and back, but Palryma took care with his molten hands to make the front of the marker as smooth as silk. He crushed a handful of the tiny pearls into powder and rubbed them into the face of the marker. It made a beautiful milky white coating. He took emeralds and pushed them way into the stone all along the border of the face of the stone. He let the tips of the emeralds show so that a shiny green string of emeralds framed the front of the marker. "And now for the name" he said as he reached for some of the rubies from the cloth carrying sack. He used his molten hands to heat them so much that they became a liquid he could pour into the letters he carved in to the stone's face. D-A-L-O, it read after he poured the red liquid into the carving. Bright red letters on a smooth face of milky white bordered by tips of shiny green. Pearls, rubies and emeralds — all to commerate the trip to the shore-by-the-sea. The place where Palryma's last words to Dalo were that he was a good guide "The very best". These were the words Palryma inscribed on the face of the burial maker just below Dalo's name:

Guide to Palryma the Chalice Maker from the village of Goosra.
The very best guide.

When he finished he went to sleep. His friends would be at the cave soon enough. But he did not go up the ladder to his own sleeping area. Instead, he lay down next to Dalo and draped his arm around him – just to be close one more time. Just this once before burial.

Morning came too early. And on this, the final day with his guide at the cave, the morning came way before Palryma wanted it to. But, he knew full well that there was no taking back of time and, yawning and stretching, sat upright next to Dalo. He peered through his still sleepy eyes at the burial marker that was placed in prominence in the middle of the work table. Palryma nodded in satisfaction at his work. It turned out quite well and he saw it as a fitting testament to his friend. Before he stood up, he leaned down and placed a quick kiss on Dalo's forehead. "I guess it is time for us to move on, by rolly-toe." he whispered. When he walked over to inspect his handiwork on the burial marker more closely, he was struck with an idea. "That's what is missing!" he shouted "I knew there should be something more!" He used his molten hands to write in one last inscription on the face of the stone. Then he stepped back and clasped his hands together. "Now it is finished!" The final inscription read:

DALO
Guide to Palryma, the Chalice Maker from the village of Goosra
The very best guide
By rolly-toe!

Palryma knew it was time to greet the day and he opened the door to the cave as wide as he could. It was a glorious and bright sunny day and he walked directly to the babbling brook to fill his bowl full of cool water. As he sipped from his bowl, he was surprised to see that only one of the three gold colored fish bobbed his head out of the water – just slightly.

"Hi Pallie. Hi." mouthed the fish ever so quietly. "We miss Dalo, too. Can we come out to say Hi?" As soon as that greeting ended, the fish dove back underneath the water. It was the first indication to Palryma that there might be others who mourned the loss of Dalo. "Of course, you can say hello" shouted Palryma into the water "I am glad to see you and happy to be back. I will be taking our friend Dalo into Goosra today." At once, all three fishes jumped out of the water.

"Hi Pallie...Hi. Hi. Hi. We missed you. We will miss Dalo. But you are still here!" After the chorus of hellos, it was right back into the brook. Palryma took another sip from his bowl and replied "I will miss Dalo, too. The shore-by-the-sea was quite a different place than the forest. I saw a whale. Biggest fish I ever saw!" Again, all three fish jumped out of the water.

"We can't have any whales in our babbling brook, Pallie! We would get squished! This water is for small fish like us, by rolly-toe! After a little bit of a dance on their fin tails all three darted right back into the water. This made Palryma laugh. The silly language lives on in the babbling brook, he thought. "Dalo would like that!"

Palryma noticed that the Kura birds were singing a bit more loudly than usual as he watched the fish jump up one more time. "Hi. Pallie" they said, "there is a visitor here, you know." Without any more information than that to go on,

Palryma assumed that the fishes saw the approach of Siglatee and Moralna. Palryma rose quickly to greet his old friends but saw no one on the dirt path at the top of the hill that led to the cave. He scratched his head and wondered what the gold colored fishes were talking about.

"Over here" said a voice "not at the top of the hill. Over here behind you."

Palryma turned towards the voice and nearly froze in silence.

"Aren't you going to say anything?"

Palryma looked but he could barely speak. Shocked by what he saw, it took a moment for him to stutter out "M...m... my...my n...n...name is P...P...Palryma. I...I...I am the Ch... Ch...Chalice Maker from G...G...Goosra."

"Oh, heavens above Mr. Palryma. I know who you are!" Yes, of course I do! And your parents are Bestra and Merrilyee. You are a chalice maker and your father used to be a cobber and you are going back to Goosra today to bury your friend, Dalo. I know all of this!"

Palryma heard the voice, but he was not sure of what he was looking at. It was some sort of being, but it was the oddest color of green and brown and had the most peculiar shape of a stick man – but a very elastic stick man. He struggled to speak to it. "Dalo is....m...m...my guide." he managed to say "who exactly are you?"

The stick man raised his stick arms and fluttered his hands that were puffy and white – almost looking like he was wearing puffy gloves. "Oh, Mr. Palryma...you are almost right. But, more correctly you should say that Dalo *was* your guide. And a very good guide he was, as I am told. A very good guide! But today you will bury him by the Shimmery Pond so it is more correct to say that Dalo *was* your guide, don't you think?"

Palryma was not pleased with this conversation and snapped "I don't think you should be talking about Dalo at all! These things don't concern you — whoever you are!"

"Ah....but Mr. Palryma, they do concern me. They concern me very much." said the stick man.

Before Palryma could think to reply the fishes jumped out of the water again. "Hi Pallie! Who is the visitor? Did you bring him from the shore-by-the-sea? He's very skinny!"

"Fishes!!!" Palryma yelled, "Please do not interrupt. It is very impolite!" But the fishes were already underneath the water and did not hear him. The stick man began to walk towards Palryma and was cautioned not to do so "You stay right where you are...do not come closer. I do not know who you are or why you are here so please take my advice and stay right where you are!"

The stick man complied and bowed his head just a bit in deference to the chalice maker. "I take your point, Mr. Palryma. Please allow me to introduce myself. I am Sum-Timmy and I am your guide."

There were no words to describe what Palryma was thinking at that introduction. He tried to say something but nothing came out of his mouth. He tried to wet his lips with water but it was no use. He could not speak. He did not want to know this stick man who claimed to be his guide. His mind was whirling in confusion and just as he raised his hand, he heard shouting from atop the hill.

"Hello and heavens above, Palryma! We made very good time getting here with Bird as our guide! How would you agree with us on that!" It was Siglatee, Moralna and Bird arriving from Goosra. They brought the litter. Palryma attempted a faint smile and wave. "What am I going to do?" he said.

Sum-Timmy smiled and waved to them. "Your friends are here, Mr. Palryma. Aren't you going to introduce me?"

Chapter Nineteen

Siglatee and Moralna greeted their childhood friend with great smiles and warm hugs. Palryma returned them in kind but was distracted nonetheless. His friends sensed that something was not right but they put it down to the tragedy of losing his guide so immediately at the shore-by-the sea. "We hurried as best we could, Palryma, as soon as Bird gave us the news." said Siglatee. "We had to gather some things first, but we were off like a shot as soon as we stopped to see your parents." added Moralna. It was the mention of his parents that snapped the chalice maker out of his confused stupor.

"How are they?" he wanted to know "How are my parents? Tell me."

"They look forward to your return but wish it were under happier circumstances. They are concerned that you not grieve heavily," explained Siglatee, "your father has already begun to dig a burial spot for your guide. He thinks you will like the spot he picked by the Shimmery Pond."

"Yes, and Bird here gave your parents all the news without delay before he came to see us. He is quite the messenger." said Moralna as he petted the sitting Bird on his shoulder. "I've become quite fond of him!"

Palryma realized that in the present whirl of welcomes he had not greeted Bird. He looked his feathered friend in the eyes and reached out his hands to him. "Sweet Lenora-ga, it is good to see you again, Bird. Come here to me." With the single flap of his wings, Bird lifted himself off of Moralna's shoulder and into Palryma's hands. Palryma brought the brave messenger up to his cheek and nuzzled him gently. "You are a savior to me Bird. Thank you for all your effort. It means the world to me."

If Bird could have blushed, he would have. Instead he just shook all his feathers. "I am always happy to help you, Sir."

"Palryma" said Moralna "may we take some water from the brook? It has been quite a journey and...."

Palryma was embarrassed at his lack of hospitality and moved to make amends. "Of course...of course my friends.... please, please drink your fill. I have sweet couldas inside the cave." Moralna dove to the edge of the brook and pulled his long red hair back with one hand so he could put his mouth directly into the water. "Moralna never wastes any time to do anything does he, Sir!" said Bird as he watched. "Not at all, Bird. You are quite right. He never has!" recalled Palryma with a smile. "I'd better get over there before he drinks the brook dry!" shouted Siglatee. Palryma knew that could not happen but decided that he'd tell his friends about the Legend of Replacements some other time. Now it was time for them both to drink their fill.

With both faces of Siglatee and Moralna nearly submerged into the cool water, the fishes leapt as high as they ever had done before out of the water. "Help! Pallie. Help! There are whales coming into our brook!" The trio fluttered atop the water before sinking into it. With no time to answer them or allay their fears, they reappeared. "Hi there Fred! Hi! Hi! Hi! We didn't see you there! Did you see the skinny man! Who are the whales?!" And then, as usual, they were gone below the surface of the water.

Moralna splashed water all over his face now that his thirst was quenched and dampened his long hair to complete the cooling process. "Who is Fred?" he asked through his bright smile.

"Oh....that's just what the fishes call Bird.....sometimes they call him Fred's brother...it just depends on how they feel!" answered Palryma "They definitely have minds of their own. You just get used to it." He walked over to the brook and stood next to his friends who were sitting cross-legged at the water's edge. "Fishes!!!" shouted Palryma into the brook "Come up here. I want you to meet my friends!!" He started to clap his hands together quickly. "Come now. Don't delay. I know you are not shy!" he teased. That was all the invitation the fishes needed.

"Hi Pallie. Hi! Hi! Hi! Hi again Fred!! Hi Pallie's friends! We are the gold colored fishes!"

"Fishes...please be calm and stay at the water level!" said Palryma. "This fine fellow here with all the long red hair and toothy grin is my old friend from Goosra, Moralna. He can run faster than almost anyone I know....except me, of course!" Palryma hopped over to crouch behind his other friend. He patted him on the shoulders as he began his introduction. "And this handsome fellow right here is Siglatee. There are those who say he is the most handsome young man in Goosra. Can you believe that?! He knows almost all of my walking songs and has a few of his own to boot." The young man with the jet blue eyes and dark black hair playfully pushed Palryma away and said "Don't you believe him fishes! Absolutely everyone knows that I *am* the most handsome young man in Goosra! Everyone!" The three young men laughed in tune with the three fishes and watched while the gold colored trio bade a swift good-bye back into the water.

"Talking birds and talking fish! This is quite a different place from Goosra, Palryma." noted Siglatee. Moralna agreed as he rose to his feet. "You don't know the half of it yet my friends" replied Palryma "not the half of it." He walked to the opening of the cave and bid them enter. "We should begin to prepare for our journey back to Goosra. Come inside."

"Aren't you forgetting something?" said the voice from behind the tree next to the wall of forgetful flowers covering the cave's door. It was Sum-Timmy.

He stepped out from behind the tree and both Siglatee and Moralna took a stance as though they were about to do battle. "Mr. Palryma, are you going to make me introduce myself? That hardly seems very polite, wouldn't you say?" Palryma rubbed his forehead and looked at his two friends. They shrugged and looked back at him not knowing exactly what to do or say. They could not imagine doing battle with this creature who looked like a stick man, but having wit-nessed several strange things since they left Goosra, they were unsure of their next move.

Palryma made it for them. "Oh, yes.....my apologies, of course. I was pre-occupied with my friends." He turned to Siglatee and Moralna and took in a long, deep breath. "Friends" he said "this....umm.....this man....err...I mean... this...this ..ahh.. fellow...yes....this fellow right here" he said gesturing to his left towards Sum-Timmy "this fellow here goes by the name of Sum-Timmy."

Siglatee and Moralna relaxed their fighting stance and dropped their arms to their sides. They looked at Sum-Timmy rather strangely and said without much conviction in their voices "Hello and heavens above to you, Sum-Timmy."

Then Siglatee took the lead. "I am Siglatee. You will know

me by my very black hair and this is my friend Moralna, who, as you can see has very long red hair. We are from Goosra and have known our good friend Palryma since we were boys."

Sum-Timmy grinned and bowed "Hello, lads. It's good to meet you. There is one important fact that Mr. Palryma left out of his introduction though...." Palryma interrupted him immediately. "I think we should get inside the cave and have something to eat....and we must begin to prepare my guide for his journey. Siglatee do you have the carrying shroud?" Siglatee nodded. "And I have the litter Palryma...I've left it just over there." added Moralna.

"Fine" said Palryma "let's begin." He motioned for his friends to enter the cave. As they complied, he took a step towards Sum-Timmy. "May I have a word in private with you?"

Sum-Timmy listened very closely as Palryma made it very clear to him that he did not want another guide. He wanted Sum-Timmy to understand that he had no need for another guide and that wherever Sum-Timmy came from he should return. He let it be known that there was never going to be anyone who could replace Dalo. Ever. Palryma sternly emphasized to Sum-Timmy that he stood very firm on this point. "Perhaps you think I am being impolite, but I must tell you that I have plans and they simply do not include you." said Palryma to the quietly observing Sum-Timmy. "I am sorry if you think me a harsh man for speaking this way, but there is no other way around it. Again, I am sorry if this has turned out to be a bit of a tangle for you, but I must be allowed to proceed with my plans. And they do not include another guide."

They stood in silence for a moment. Palryma thought it best to say nothing more. He had made his point and he was allowing time for it to register with Sum-Timmy. Sum-

Timmy, on the other hand, knew exactly what he was going to say....what he had to say, but was wondering just how he was going to say it. He did not want to give offense or frighten Palryma off. He started very slowly by clasping his white, puffy hands together in front of him.

"Mr. Palryma, I understand what you are trying to say. I feel deeply for your circumstance. But, I too, must be direct even if it appears to you that I do not understand. But, believe me, I do." He continued with a bit more confidence. "I am not here of my own accord. I have been sent to you — much the same way that your beloved Dalo was sent to you."

Palryma seemed shocked at this suggestion but fully intended not to veer from his stated position. "What do you mean you were "sent" here?"

"It was Batoowa who sent me here. It is Batoowa, himself, who has decided that you shall continue to have a guide and that guide, by his very own decision, is to be me." Palryma tried to recollect the day of his initiation rite when he first met Batoowa but his memory of that day only recalled the wedding celebration of his parents –- and meeting Dalo for the first time. He had not heard from or seen Batoowa since that day. Sum-Timmy could see that Palryma was deeply thinking on that day and on his initiation rite and offered this hint at recollection. "Do you remember, after the initiation rite was over, and you were in the road that lead back to Goosra with your Shatoo birds and your firewood?"

Palryma spoke with some hesitation about that day. "I....I...don't really have...you know...don't have...a great...I mean...I don't really have a good recollection of...of the initiation rite at all. I...I...thought...that...well....actually...I thought that it might...you know....come back to me...sort of....well, that I'd get....I mean I'd remember it better in time. But that has not happened and frankly....well...to tell the truth....I have had many things....many other things happen since then...that it....well it all seems such a blur."

The look on Sum-Timmy's face spoke volumes about Palryma's experience. "Most new chalice makers have a bit of difficulty remembering the exact details. You shouldn't let it concern you. You will recollect it all in time. I can help you remember it, if you like."

"What do you mean? Were you there." said the dubious chalice maker.

Sum-Timmy explained "Well...I wasn't actually present at the initiation rite itself...at least not yours! But, I know all about it. Everyone heard all about it. Yours was very special – very particular to you but I have been at others. They are all a little different from one another and all very exquisite. I must say that we all thought yours was quite colorful and cheerful – quite like the new chalice maker, himself! Wouldn't you say? Or, how is it that you express it in Goosra: "How would you agree with me on that?"

Palryma was stunned – almost speechless. "You were there on the day I was chosen to be a chalice maker?" was all he could think of to say. "Oh yes...on the day you were cho-sen and on the day that others have been chosen as well. It's a beautiful ceremony and because it doesn't happen all that often, we all like to watch, if we can. We'd all like to be pres-ent but that is not possible but we all eventually hear about it and all the details sooner or later" answered Sum-Timmy.

Palryma shook his head in wonderment "How many were watching?"

"Oh...the numbers aren't important. What's important is that you continue to learn the ways of a chalice maker and I have been chosen as your guide to help you accomplish exactly that." Feeling much more relaxed now, Sum-Timmy continued. "That is why I asked you earlier if you remembered what Batoowa told you right after the ceremony was over."

Palryma shook his head. "I just don't remember...perhaps if you could help me." Hearing this, the grin on Sum-Timmy's face was memorable. "Oh...I be so happy to help you for this is my job!" Right then and there it became apparent to Palryma that this stick man named Sum-Timmy had no intentions of leaving. It became clear to him that he was going to have to back off from his stance that he had no need of another guide.

"I will tell you exactly what happened for my memory is excellent. I have a real talent for remembering details of events no matter how long ago they occurred" said the excited Sum-Timmy. "You were standing in the middle of the road — a bit confused, I might add! — but who wouldn't be after an initiation rite like that! Anyway, what you said to Batoowa was this:

"Will I just sit and wait to hear from you?"

"Do you remember saying that?" he asked Palryma. "Not really" was the answer.

"No matter. But trust me, that is what you said. My memory is excellent on this point. Let me tell you what Batoowa's reply was. Maybe you will remember that. He said:

"Do not worry for your guides will be along by and by."

"Any recollection of that?" Again, Palryma shook his head. "Sorry. I just can't remember it...at least not right now."

"Toffle and too! Think nothing of it. It will come to you. But what is most important, Mr. Palryma, is that Batoowa used the word "guides". Plural. You see it was always meant, from the beginning, that you would have more than one guide. On this, Mr. Palryma, you will have no say. It is Batoowa's decision. Not yours. Best not to question it."

"I see what you mean," said Palryma with a hint of res-ignation in his voice. He struggled for more words. "You are here," he said to Sum-Timmy "but what are you going to do? I already know how to make chalices. Dalo taught me that."

"And, might I add, he did an excellent job of it." replied Sum-Timmy. "But that is only part of it. I am here to show you more."

"More what?" questioned Palryma

"More of the *ways* of a chalice maker, Mr. Palryma. The making of the chalices is only the beginning. You have much to learn yet." A sudden weariness came over Palryma. "Why can't I stop now? Why can't I just go back now and live in Goosra? Why must I go on? I miss my friends and my parents. I would very much like to marry Allura Rose. Why can't you just come back with me to Goosra and show me the rest of the "ways" back there?"

Sum-Timmy knew that Palryma had not had time to properly mourn Dalo's death and that he was anxious about things to come. He wanted to put his mind at ease but did not want to give him expectations of things that were not going to happen. "It's not the way things are done when you are a chalice maker, Mr. Palryma. You may certainly have all those things you mentioned, but not at this time. There are things you must yet do. I'll ask of you the very same thing that Dalo asked of you when you first met. Have faith in me, Mr. Palryma. I mean you no harm. I have been given a job to do and that job is to be your guide."

"Guide me to what? I just don't understand," was Palryma's reply.

"Well....I cannot tell you everything. But, I will tell you that the very first thing I have been directed to do is to take you to see Great Ben!"

Now this time Palryma was truly speechless. He knew that Great Ben was the most reknown and revered chalice maker in the land. His very name was utterly legendary and his chalices were sought after from far and wide. No one had seen him in years; in fact, there were those in the land who thought he had long since died. No one knew where he lived. Palryma began to hear about Great Ben when he was just a boy from the tales his grandfather, Wilyatam, told him. He just assumed that the Great Chalice Maker saw no one. The rumors about his chalices fit every size and shape of every imagination possible. Palryma laughed at the remembrance of the scheme that he, Siglatee and Moralna cooked up when they were eight years old. They planned to creep up to the Castle of Hurrah III and sneak in to take away the chalice made by Great Ben that was rumored to be inside. They were going to return with it to Goosra and become the heroes of the village. "Every girl in the village will want to kiss us!" exclaimed Siglatee, who at eight years old was already show-ing signs of becoming impossibly handsome "this is truly a great plan!" Unfortunately, the plan was foiled when Bestra found the crude map drawn up by the three young would-be adventurers because Palryma left it lying on top of one of his books as he fell asleep next to the warm fireplace in his house. Needless to say, the boys never executed their plan. An appro-priate punishment was executed by their fathers, but not the plan. It remained something they all agreed that they would put off 'till another time — when they were older and could run faster.

Palryma always thought it was a good plan and now des-tiny, in an odd, strained turn, seemed to favor what remained of the the sentiment of the boys' plan — to see one of Great

Ben's chalices. But it was only to be Palryma in charge of the execution this time.

"You actually know Great Ben...I mean you have met him before?" said Palryma.

"Oh yes...I have known him for quite a long time. After all, I am 9,000 years old!"

Palryma nearly fainted. "This is too much for me to take in all at once." he said to Sum-Timmy.

"Toffle and too, Mr. Palryma. Toffle and too! There is no need for you to take it in all at once. Besides, I am here to help you do all that. What you should do is first things first. Your friends await you in the cave. There is much to do before you carry Dalo back to Goosra. You must get started. It will take you several long hours to walk back and then there must be the burial ceremony and, of course, you will want to have a short visit with your parents. I think you should meet me at the edge of the wet fields, just outside Goosra in exactly one day and a half, to be precise. From there we will go to meet Great Ben."

"You seem to have this all planned out, Sum-Timmy."

"Thank you for noticing! It's one of the things I do best – plan things out, that is. I always have a plan!"

"All right, I guess I will have to trust you. Dalo would want that."

"Wonderful!! See how easy that was! Now you take that wheeled cart behind you and put Dalo's burial stone in it. It will make things easier for you."

Palryma looked around in back of him and cocked his head as he looked again at Sum-Timmy. "How did that get there?"

"I made it appear," replied Sum-Timmy with a smile. "I can do things like that because that's the kind of guide I am!

You didn't think that I was going to let you carry the heavy burial stone all the way back to Goosra did you, now? I think that was your plan. But I think now you prefer my plan!"

"Well" said Palryma sheepishly "my plan was to have Siglatee and Moralna take turns in carrying it with me."

"So....your friends can thank me later. Go now. They are waiting for you. I will see you in exactly one day and a half."

And then, right before Palryma's very eyes, Sum-Timmy disappeared.

The chalice maker headed inside the cave to be with his friends, Siglatee, Moralna, Bird and, of course, Dalo. All together for the first and last time.

Chapter Twenty

It would have been unlike the three friends from Goosra to prepare Dalo's body for the litter in silence. It was a rare occasion, indeed, when the three of them were together that anything, in fact, was done in silence. To be sure, they were respectful enough that they were getting ready to carry Dalo back to Goosra, but that did not mean they would carry this task out under unnatural vocal restrictions. That would have been too much to ask of them.

Moralna was a tale-teller and reveled in his ability to enthrall and enrapture a crowd, however small, with well put-together words. Humor was Moralna's strength and his natural sense of it was the characteristic in him that Palryma admired most. Siglatee was a complete charmer and had an ability to talk to anyone about almost anything. Engaging to a fault, Siglatee talked so much that he often could not remember just what he said to whom and just where he said it. Combined with his dark good looks, this penchant of his for charming displays of loquaciousness often landed him in awkward corners with his girlfriends. All it took was one exasperated look from either Moralna or Palryma and Siglatee knew right away that his ramblings should come to a quick end. The friendship among them had endured for years. When they were but five years old they vowed to be friends to the end. On this point they never wavered. It would have been unthinkable. They treated each other as brothers.

Palryma was the fearless one, though. Both Siglatee and Moralna recognized this in him. He was a good talker, but not the tale-teller that Moralna was and he was definitely charming, but did not hold sway with girls the way Siglatee did. They shared their admirable qualities with each other freely and thusly, made perfect compliments to each other. Three peas in a pod.

But, only one was a chalice maker and rather than any untoward display of envy at the event, both Siglatee and Moralna were proud in knowing that the new chalice maker was their forever friend. They were always at such ease with each other and never once exchanged a crossword.

So, it was fitting that they worked hand in hand in moving Dalo from his sleeping area on to the worktable. They all proceeded very carefully in placing him into the white shroud that was quickly hand-made by Merrilyee upon hearing the news from Bird that her only son would be returning to Goosra with his guide. She even packed into a small sack the large needle and heavy cotton thread that would be needed to sew Dalo's shroud up forever. Merrilyee paid attention to the smallest of details. She always did. When she gave the items to Moralna she said "Make sure you tell my son that his mother awaits to help him through this bad time."

Moralna was intrigued by the chalices that Palryma had in varying stages of completion on the worktable. Siglatee could not help but notice his friend's cloth carrying case, lying on the floor of the cave, filled with tiny pearls, emeralds and rubies from the shore-by-the-sea. They were both terribly impressed with the burial stone Palryma made for Dalo. They were filled with question after question and Palryma told his friends all he could about everything that had happened to him since he left Goosra. He told them all about Dalo and why he decided to have his burial in Goosra. But he really had only one thing on his mind: Allura Rose. He simply had to get word to her before he left for Goosra. He thought of trying to meet up with her briefly in the forest before they left but there was no time now. It was approaching mid-day and if they were to get Dalo back to Goosra before night-fall they had to leave soon. Moralna suggested that Palryma wait until after the burial ceremony when he returned to the cave before rushing to see Allura Rose. "That is, of course, if you can wait that long!" he teased, "For it seems that you are learning more than the ways of a chalice maker out here!" The red-haired taleteller did not know about Sum-Timmy's plan to take Palryma to meet Great Ben. Palryma thought best to leave it that way.

"No....no....I must find a way to get word to her that I have returned from the shore-by-the sea. I must let her know that I have not forgotten about her." Then he was struck with what he thought was a whale of an idea.

"Bird!!!" he shouted "Are you able to take on another mes-senger assignment for me?"

"At your command, Sir! I am ready whenever you are!" was the reply.

"You are the only one here who knows exactly where my love goes to pick her forest flowers. And she knows you well.... likes you quite well. In fact, didn't you tell me that you and she got along very nicely when last you met?"

"We did exactly that, Sir! Rosie and Dalo and I had a good, fun time altogether."

"Then could you....would you do this for me, Bird? Bring a message to her. Let her know what has happened and that I will see her again as soon as I can."

"It would be my pleasure, Sir!"

"Perhaps I should accompany Bird on this assignment" volunteered the handsome Siglatee "just to take care that he does not get lost."

"Sir!!!"squeeled Bird.

"Siglatee....Bird knows this part of the forest better than any of us. Rest assured that he will not get lost...will you Bird?"

"Never, Sir!"

"Besides, Siglatee, do you think I will allow you to meet my love without my being there to make the introduction? That would be a little impolite, don't you think?" he said with a wink.

Moralna laughed at the very thought of Siglatee on the loose in the forest looking for Palryma's new love. "Wise decision, Palryma. Very wise." he added with a mock seriousness.

"Very well then, it's settled. Bird will fly off to Allura Rose with my message and we three — emphasis on *three*, I add — will take Dalo back to Goosra. Oh...and Bird....can you carry this in your beak?" Palryma reached down to his cloth carrying sack and picked out a beautiful tiny pearl and held it up for Bird to see. "Yes, Sir...I can carry that to Rosie!"

"You won't swallow it now will you?" teased the chalice maker.

"Not to worry, Sir!"

"Good. And then meet up with us in Goosra when you are finished. Come to my parents' home. We will be waiting for you." Bird agreed to fly as fast as his wings would carry him.

"Then we are off!" declared Palryma

"Sir" said Bird. Palryma looked at him as to wonder why he wasn't out the cave door yet. "What is it, Bird?' he asked.

"Not to be impolite, Sir....but the message, Sir. What exactly is the message that you want me to deliver to Rosie?"

"Well...you know...just that we are taking Dalo back to Goosra for burial....explain to her without too much detail, if you know what I mean, about what happened at the shore-by-the sea and that I will return to see her just as soon as I can."

"That's all, Sir? Nothing about the pearl that I will drop into her hand?"

"Hmmmm.....I guess you are right, Bird." Palryma bent over to Bird, cupped his hands around his tiny head and whis-pered something. "Tell her that!"

"Yes, Sir. I will! That is a very important part of the mes-sage!" Palryma placed Bird on his arm and walked to the open door of the cave. "Off with you now! Come back to me safely."

He turned to see his friends sitting at the worktable smil-ing at him. "What was it that you whispered?" They both asked. "You will learn soon enough." was his reply. Siglatee slammed his hand down on the table and shouted "Sweet Lenora-ga, Moralna! I think we shall soon have a happy cel-ebration in Goosra! How would you agree with me on that?"

"Siglatee...I would agree with you in every way possible. In every way possible!"

"You both get ahead of yourselves. We have an important task at hand. We should get started."

With Siglatee at the front of the litter and Moralna at the back they began to move up the hill outside the cave. Palryma was right behind them pushing the wheel cart that carried Dalo's burial stone. And so the long funeral procession back to Goosra had finally begun.

"These friends of Palryma's...I think they are very good

for him." said one of the Kura birds as they watched the procession move out of sight.

"Do you think he will return?" said the smallest of them all.

"In time he will" said the oldest of the Kura birds "when he learns a few more things...for he is a chalice maker now."

Chapter Twenty-One

Bird was not long in flying to the spot in the forest where Palryma first met Allura Rose. The beautiful forest flowers that she loved so much were all in bloom but Allura Rose was nowhere to be found. Bird nestled himself into a corner branch nook of one of the Loofa-nally trees – just high enough to give him a good view of the glen where she might appear. The Loofa-nally trees had big, red and brown leaves shaped like cups so Bird deposited the tiny pearl he was to give to Palryma's love into the nearest leaf to his resting spot. Alone in the tree, he reflected for a moment on the monumental changes his life had undergone since the chalice maker found him nearly dead under the patch of forgetful flowers not so very long ago – and not too very far away from the very spot where he waited and watched. He knew full well from his time as Settela in the service of Hurrah III that the dark-as-night-flying Reelatta horses would not forget that one of their own had been killed in the murderous attack on Dalo at the shore-by-the-sea. He always thought that vengeance flowed hotly through the blood of those horses at the direction of their mighty ruler. "They will not soon forget that one of their own was caused to drop into the depths of the ocean – blinded by some flying bird." he thought quietly "whether they recognized me in the dark of the night, I cannot say but they surely as I sit in this Loofa-nally tree, I know they reported the attack to Hurrah III. I used to do the same type of reporting myself and the vengeance of Hurrah knows no bounds. I will discuss this matter with Sir when I arrive in Goosra later. But for now, I will have a small rest and wait for Rosie." Bird's eyelids grew droopy and soon enough he was taking his well-deserved nap in the forest.

With his eyes closed he was, naturally, unable to see the lovely forest girl, Allura Rose, waltz gracefully down the dirt path with a basket only half-full of her favorite sweet forest flowers. Lovlier than ever, she managed to effortlessly sway to and fro as she decided which of the flowers would be selected to make the day's bouquet for her grandmother. It was the lilt of her singing that eventually woke Bird.

"Rosie!" he peeped, "It is I...Bird!!" She looked around to locate the sound of her friend.

"I'm up here in the Loofa-nally tree! I can see you very well!" A bright smile from her told Bird that he had been spotted and he began to flap his wing for a descent. Rosie's welcome was not disappointing. She was legitimately glad to see Bird once again and offered her lap for him to lie in. "My sweet Bird!" she exclaimed "what a joy to see you safe and sound back from your adventure to the shore-by-the-sea." Bird looked up at her with anticipation at what he must say about the adventure and could not help but notice again how simply beautiful she was.

"Oh, Rosie there are so many things I must tell you. Our big adventure did not end well, I am afraid."

Allura Rose did not respond directly but the look that came over her flawless face was one that assured Bird that she was listening to his every word. The look in her eyes told Bird that she wanted to know everything about what now seemed apparently to have been mis-adventure. Bird did not hold back. He told her everything.

At the end of his sad telling Allura Rose was very silent. Her first expression thereafter was for the well being of Palryma. The single tear in the corner of her eye was the solitary indication that she was gutted by the ghastly scenario that ended Dalo's life.

"I cannot believe that Dalo is gone from us." she said without looking at Bird. "His heart was so big and generous. He was so very fond of Palryma. You were very brave, Bird, to fly to his rescue."

"It was awful Rosie," recalled Bird "and Sir was sadder than any young man I have ever seen. It broke my heart to hear the sounds of him endlessly weeping."

Rose pulled her flaxen hair to one side and wiped away the single tear in her eye. "I know one thing for certain, Bird" she said without a quiver in her voice "Palryma has the strength of Honalee giants. He will survive this loss, Bird and he will be all the stronger for it. Rest assured of this."

"I hope you are right, Rosie. I hope you are right." Allura Rose stroked his feathers with a touch that convinced Bird that she was solid in her belief in Palryma's strength. "Oh my!" he said "I almost forgot something!!" He flapped his wings to carry him upwards to the cupped leaf in the Loofa-nally tree where the tiny pearl rested. Picking it up in his beak, he practically floated back down to drop it in her palm. "It is a present, Rosie, from Sir. He collected it at the shore-by-the-sea when we first arrived." Allura Rose saw the pearl as the completion of Palryma's promise to bring her back some-thing special. The tiny pearl was a token of his love and she recognized it as exactly that. "It comes with a message too, Rosie! Do you want to hear it?"

"But of course, Bird! Are not messages meant to be heard!?" she teased. "Tell me what my love wants me to know." She bent her head down so Bird could whisper the message in her ear. When he was finished, Bird exclaimed "Pretty nice message, isn't it Rosie!?"

"There could be none better, Bird." she replied with a bit of blush now in her cheeks.

Bird and Rosie spent the next few hours talking and picking flowers. She would point at a flower too distant or too high for her to reasonably reach and Bird would fly to it and pluck it up with his beak. "My grandmother will wonder how I got so many unusual forest flowers on my trip today. These pink and yellow cup-de-cups are just lovely and I have never been able to reach them on my own!"

"Will you tell her that your friend Bird helped you collect your flowers today, Rosie?"

"I will most certainly tell her that, Bird. In fact, I will tell her that it was your idea to make the flower arrangement so full of new and beautiful forest flowers."

"What's she like.....your grandmother, I mean. Is she a nice lady?

"Oh...she is the most wonderful lady I know, Bird." said Allura Rose without hesitation. Then she added "I have an idea Bird. Why don't you come with me to meet her this very afternoon? I'm certain that she will be very pleased to meet you! I think she probably has never met a talking bird before....although with my grandmother you never can know!" she added with a twinkle. "You could fly to Goosra tomorrow morning after a restful night."

Bird needed only a moment to think about the very welcoming invitation. He could tell that the afternoon sky was getting heavy with an azure blue tint which meant that the forest would soon be dark in a couple of hours. If he was going to arrive in Goosra before the sun disappeared altogether, he knew he had to leave quite soon. But he was having such a lovely time with Allura Rose that he could not come to an immediate decision. "Is your home a far distance from here, Rosie?" he asked looking for some way to accept her invitation.

"Oh, no...not at all. Why I am always able to make it to this spot to collect my flowers from my home in less time than it takes to recite aloud the 12 Legends of Sweet Lenora-ga!"

"Hmmmm...." replied Bird thoughtfully "not to be impolite or anything, as Sir would say, Rosie but that doesn't mean too much to me. I never learned those 12 legends as a little chirper!"

Allura Rose laughed aloud and shook her basket of flowers, in mock reprimand, which was now full and atop which Bird was comfortable nestled. "Well then, I will just have to tell you them myself, won't I? They are all so interesting and so exciting to hear! It takes me about a half and hour to recite them. I learned them by heart when I was only six years old!"

A strong wind picked up just as she was speaking and the azure blue tint in the sky above began to swirl around and rise higher – a sure sign that it was quickly leaving to make room for the night sky. Bird knew if he was leaving it had to be now. Flying to Goosra would not be easy in this wind. "I think I will have to meet your grandmother when we all return from Goosra after Dalo's burial. I promised Sir that I would meet him at the home of his parents this evening and I like to keep my promises."

"Of course, I understand, Bird. We will all have a grand meeting altogether at another time." she assured him "and you are right...promises are meant to be kept so you'd best be on your way if you want to be in Goosra before dark. I think this sudden wind will bring the night sky in more quickly that we think!"

"Yes, indeed" said Bird "and I do not like to fly at night!"

— "at all" he added with emphasis.

"Then off you go! But before you leave may I give you a message to deliver to my handsome chalice maker?" Bird nodded most enthusiastically and Allura Rose lowered her lips to whisper it to him. Before she drew away, she gave Bird a small kiss on the top of his head.

Bird looked surprised and said "You don't want me to kiss him too, do you!!?"

"No Bird. That kiss was for you!"

The flutter of his wings covered Bird's embarrassment and as he began to rise higher in the sky he shouted "Goodbye, Rosie my friend!!! Be safe. I will see you soon!"

The strong winds were lifting Bird higher and higher but he could still see the beautiful forest girl, Allura Rose, waving goodbye.

"Good fortune will still come to Sir — even after the events at the shore-by-the-sea" thought Bird as he made steady course for Goosra and fought the ever-increasing winds. "Rosie will bring Sir good fortune."

Perhaps.

But it was not Palryma who needed good fortune right now. It was Bird. He noticed that the night sky seemed to be chasing him with a vengeance to Goosra — what he did not notice was the trio of dark-as-night flying Reelatta horses following him.

Bird was flying against time. He flapped his wings with all the strength he had and glided when he thought he could ride the wind. He was staying just ahead of the disappearing azure sky and thought he might just make it to Goosra before nightfall with a little luck. He decided to fly higher hoping to get above of the heady wind that was proving to be a challenge for him. He rose higher and higher until he was in the thick of the azure tint which made flying easier but the color made his visibility difficult. "I don't need to see the ground" he assured himself "I could find Goosra with my eyes closed." This confident affirmation did not belay the fact that Bird did not, and never did, like flying at night. This dislike had been with him for years. Bird always liked to be home before dark. Today was no different. After a while of flying high in the azure tint, Bird decided to descend again to test the winds. He brought his wings close to his side and dove like a bombardier back into the wind. It was a trick his father taught him, but one, he was warned, that required "nerve to burn" as his father so often aptly demonstrated. If there was one thing Bird had plenty of as a young chipper, it was "nerve to burn." He had so little fear.

This lack of fear was a good thing because when Bird emerged from the azure tint, he found himself only a few flaps ahead of the three dark-as-night flying Reelatta horses who were furtively searching the approaching night sky for him. He was immediately spotted and just as immediately Bird knew he was directly in harm's way. With one flap of their huge wings, the horses began to converge upon Bird. They were so close that Bird could hear the sound of their wings flapping.

"Do you think you can catch me!!!?" Bird shouted as he flapped his own wings furiously. "Do you think I will allow you to take me back to that wretched castle? Never!!" The horses needed only one more flap of their wings to pounce upon Bird and he'd be done for. "Don't you remember that I used to fly with you? Don't you remember that I was Settela!!" he shouted back at them. He could practically hear them breathing. "I remember plenty about you! I remember that you cannot do this!!!"

With that, Bird brought his wings tight to his side and went immediately into a deep bombardier dive straight towards the ground with no inclination to stop. "Follow me now!!" he taunted. "I dare you to follow me now!!"

Furious that they had been challenged by someone so much smaller than them and fearful that Hurrah III would beat them if they returned without a captured Bird, the two largest horses foolishly took Bird up on his dare. They attempted to copy the carefully executed bombardier dive and it resulted in disaster for them. As soon as they brought their huge wings to their side their flight came to a dead stop. They were too big, too heavy, to glide or ride the wind. The force and speed of their fall through the sky prevented any attempt to re-spread their wings. Both of them went hurdling to the ground never to be heard from again. The only thing Bird could see when he flew out of his own bombardier dive was one, lone dark-as-night flying Reelatta horse in the distance who had wisely decided not to follow his fellow horses into a death dive. This horse had obviously decided to stop chasing after Bird and was slowly flying away – apparently lost in the sky.

"He's not headed back to the castle, that's for sure – it's in the opposite direction. I wonder where he's headed." Bird felt lucky that the lone surviving horse was no longer chasing him as he was getting very tired and night had already started to fall.

But fortunately he could see the village of Goosra just off in the distance. He'd be at the home of Bestra and Merrilyee in no time. He'd have kept his promise to Palryma to arrive at his side before nightfall.

"Home before dark!" Bird sang "Always best to be home before dark!"

Chapter Twenty-Two

The next morning found the kitchen at the home of Bestra and Merrilyee fuller than it had been since the night of their wedding celebration. Their son, now the chalice maker, was home and Merrilyee, especially, was grateful. It was not important how temporary the return would be. However, she could see that there was something changed, something unidentifiable, about her beautiful son but there was also a comfort in her soul that still saw the delightful boy in whom she and her husband took so much parental pride.

Some yards distant from the kitchen window's view, Bestra dug the grave into which his son wished to place his departed guide, Dalo. It was respectfully removed from the often-busy comings and goings of the cottage he built for his family, but not so far that it could not be gazed upon with ease. Palryma was happy with the spot his father selected. It was almost the same spot where he excitedly plunged into the Shimmery Pond nearly twenty years earlier when he first learned to swim. It had since become his favorite spot to sit and think about things. Dalo's presence there would now bring the chalice maker great solace and comfort. Over the years, the Shimmery Pond had taught Palryma many things about swimming and life, in general, and Dalo had taught him invaluable lessons about chalice making and life altogether. It was fitting that Dalo's remains shared such an important piece of ground to Palryma. When he was at the Shimmery Pond he only thought of the good things that could happen in life and he wanted to hold that sentiment true when he thought of Dalo. Dalo resting in peace beside the Shimmery Pond was a good idea.

The burial ceremony was brief. Palryma's lifelong friends, Siglatee and Moralna, placed Dalo's body in the ground. Bestra and Beeloma the Baker shoveled the dirt in to cover it. When the first mound of dirt hit Dalo's lifeless body, Palryma's knees weakened. It was almost too much for him to bear to watch his colorful friend being covered up with dry, almost colorless dirt. Merilyee could see that the burial process was causing her son to quiver slightly and she moved ever so carefully next to him to take hold of his hand. She was, as ever, a most steadying influence in her son's life.

"It is only his body, Palryma. Nothing more." his mother whispered sweetly "His spirit soared away at the shore-by-the sea. Let him go. Let him continue to soar. Your love is strength enough to give him wings. Perhaps, with the grace of Sweet Lenora-ga, he will come back to you one day." Palryma tightened his grasp on her hand and nodded solemnly.

"You have been chosen by the gods. Your job is to go on living. It would be a disappointment to your guide if you stopped now." Without looking up, Palryma nodded silently again.

When Bestra and Belooma completed their task of covering the grave, Palryma stood forth to lift the burial marker from the wheeled cart. He moved it with ease and knelt to place it firmly at the head of the grave. It took only a few moments for him to firmly place the base of the burial marker in the ground forever. And within moments, all attendants at the grave began to hear the loveliest, sweetest sound fill the air. They all looked up to see from where this beautiful sound came. Palryma recognized it instantly and spotted them a few yards away atop one of the tallest Surrupta trees at the Shimmery Pond. It was the Kura birds. They left their perch above the cave in the forest and flew to Palryma's home to pay tribute to Dalo. Their symphonic sound was the best Palryma had ever heard them sing and he gave them a big wave as he stood. Their glorious sound lifted everyone's spirits. Bird, who had been sitting on Palryma's shoulder throughout the entire ceremony, began to chirp along, taking pride in the fact that his fellow birds-of-a-feather were bringing smiles to sullen faces.

Simmee-Sammy, the village historian gladly recorded all of this in his big Book of Events.

Everyone remarked at the beauty of the burial marker that Palryma made. They knew nothing of the power of a chalice maker's molten hands and marveled at the strength and delicacy of its carving and design.

"What an extraordinary monument you have made for Dalo" declared Bethnee, the bakers wife. Siglatee's mother could not get over how shiny the rubies and emeralds were. "What beautiful treasures, Palryma." she said "I, myself, was told as a very young girl that treasures abound at the shore-by-the-sea and now you bring us all proof of it! What a fitting memorial for your friend."

Palryma accepted all the various compliments in stride but knew in his heart that he would trade them all in for Dalo's return.

After the burial ceremony was complete, the gathering inside the home of Bestra and Merilyee was not quite as solemn. Certainly, the villagers paid respects to the chalice maker and his late guide. Each was touching in their own way. Some were sadder than others. Billora's father, Pantara, told Palryma that, even after all these years, he was still never able to bring himself to create a burial place for his long-lost son.

"It would pain me greatly to think that I have buried the spirit of my beloved Billora. I could not bear it if I thought he was lost to me forever. Every single day as I make my fishing nets, I pray to Sweet Lenora-ga that my son finds his way back to Goosra and his loving father." Pantara said meekly "If he had only not tried to find a cure for my blindness in Latima he might still be a chalice maker today. Alas, he is gone these many years from my home and my protective arms."

"Latima was always known to us all as a very bad place, Pantara." said Palryma as he comforted him. "Think of how much love he must have had for his father to risk such an excursion. We can only hope that Sweet Lenora-ga answers your prayers."

"You are the new chalice maker, Palryma. Can you do anything to help me find my boy? Can you use your powers as a chalice maker to bring him back to me?" Pantara asked through his sightless eyes.

"I am only just learning the ways of a chalice maker, my neighbor. I still have much to learn. I can only join you in your messages to Sweet Lenora-ga." was the only adequate reply Palryma could think of to say.

"Whatever you can do to help. I will be in your debt" the old man said as he sadly walked away on the arm of Acutra, his wife who had been unable to utter one single sound since Billora disappeared many years ago.

Bestra took notice that his son had been standing for hours – since early dawn, in fact, and motioned for him to join him at the table near the big fire at the back of the house. "Come Palryma. Come join your father" he shouted.

When Palryma approached the table he saw that Bird was sitting at the edge of it chatting with Bestra. "And what tales, may I ask, are you two exchanging in my absence?!" he teased.

"I think Bird, here, is the one with all the tales, my son! How would you agree with me on that?" Bestra smiled.

"I'm afraid I would have to agree with you in every way possible, father. Yes, indeed. In every way possible! Bird truly does have some very interesting tales to tell!"

"Sir!!!" squealed Bird "I wasn't telling any tales, to be sure!" He rose to his feet and wiggled his white tail. "Why, I was only telling your wonderful father here all about Rosie!"

The blush in Palryma's cheeks could have filled an entire morning sky in Goosra.

"And a very nice tale Bird has to tell about this lovely Allura Rose, I must say." answered Bestra with an arched eyebrow "Have you decided at the age of 23 to start keeping important information from your mother and me?"

Palryma felt quite awkward and pleaded that this was truly not the case. "No...no, father. Never! I was going to tell you and mother about her after the guests had all gone home. It's just that I considered the information to be private" he said as he stared at Bird.

"Too late, Sir!!" said Bird with a happy chirp "I already told your father everything! Including how beautiful Rosie is!" Bestra was bellowing with laughter. "And you must agree, Sir, mustn't you?'

"Agree with what, Bird?" responded an exasperated and somewhat embarrassed Palryma.

"That Rosie is indeed quite beautiful, Sir!"

Just the mention of her beauty was enough to take Palryma's breath away. It rendered him speechless.

"Hmmmmmm..." said Bestra as he stroked his chin for it was not often that he ever remembered his son rendered speechless. "So Palryma.....how would you agree with Bird on that?"

The young chalice maker drew a deep breath and smiled broadly as he gazed into the sky with his violet eyes. Then he shouted "I would agree with Bird in every way possible, father! She is the most beautiful girl I have ever seen!"

The shouting and commotion drew Merrilyee's attention and she began to walk out from the kitchen. "Heavens above! It sounds like there is news afloat out here. How would you agree with me on that, Bestra?"

"Better ask your son, my love!"

"I have met the most beautiful girl in the world, mother! Her name is Allura Rose and I am going to marry her!!" yelped Palryma

"So that was it" Merrilyee thought quietly to herself. "That's what is different with my son. That's the unidentifiable quality I noticed right away. My son is in love. We have a silver lining to our day now. Joy has come here this afternoon where sadness enveloped us this morning."

"What better news for a mother to hear than her son has truly found the girl of his dreams!" she replied with open arms. "Come inside here and tell me all about this wonderful girl. We will have cardboard seed tea and toady bread with white frosting. Come now, Palryma. Come inside and tell me all about your love!"

Father and son, with Bird perched on Palryma's arm, walked inside beckoned by the lady of the house.

And no one noticed that as they strolled inside to talk about Allura Rose that a circle of Cannerello Cupid flowers suddenly sprouted up around Dalo's grave.

It seemed like everyone was very happy to hear the news!

Chapter Twenty-Three

"I told you so! Didn't I say so when we were in the cave?!" said Siglatee to Moralna. "Didn't I say that we would be having a wedding right here in Goosra in no time at all!" Siglatee was puffed with enthusiasm with the official news and strutting like a Kura bird with the notion that he was right all along. "Oh...our friend Palryma may have tried to fool us and put us off, but I knew....I knew by the look on his face when he spoke of her that he was a young man in love!" Siglatee reached for his cup of cardboard seed tea and raised it towards his childhood friend "All the blessings of Sweet Lenora-ga upon you and your lovely Allura Rose, Palryma! Moralna and I are delighted with your happiness...aren't we Moralna?" Moralna nodded in ready agreement that his delight with the news was indeed genuine. "You have been a great friend to me all my life, Palryma. I look forward to the day when the gods in your chalice maker line bring you and Allura Rose together for eternity! Blessings of Sweet Lenora-ga upon you both!"

"Thank you my friends." answered Palryma with a broad grin "It will be a special day for both my love and I when you both are standing next to us at the ceremony of marriage love – witnesses to my pledge of eternal love." Siglatee and Moralna raised their arms in grateful acknowledgement of Palryma's invitation to be a part of the ceremony of marriage love. "We will be there, chalice maker! We will wear our finest hunting gear on that day!" they shouted in unison.

The villager friends still gathered in the home of Bestra and Merrilyee sang songs and sipped cardboard seed tea and generally reveled in the great news that the chalice maker had decided to wed. Many stories of Palryma as a young boy were swapped back and forth and everyone wished the blessings of Sweet Lenora-ga upon him. Everyone was glad that the sadness of Dalo's burial had passed and was now replaced with the joy of wedding news.

In between all the handshakes and kisses from the villagers, Palryma managed to relay the story of his first meeting with Allura Rose to both his parents – little piece by little piece. "If we can be as happy as you both are" he said to his parents "I think our lives will be complete."

"Oh, Sir!!" interrupted Bird "Oh Sir...in the ceremony and excitement of the day I forgot something. I was overwhelmed with the day's events and it slipped my mind entirely. Please forgive me."

"What's to forgive, Bird? It truly has been a busy day and we are all a bit tired. You must be especially tired from your flight into Goosra last night. One could easily understand if something slipped your mind. Think nothing of it."

"But Sir! It is very important...I have a message from Rosie for you!"

Palryma immediately put Bird on his arm and started to walk out the back door. "Come with me" he said not waiting for Bird's acquiescence. When they were away from the crowd still milling around in the cottage he looked at Bird rather sternly. "How could you forget something as important as that?" Bird lowered his head. "I am truly sorry Sir. It's just that with burial ceremony this morning and now your nice news of wedding intentions and all these nice people here...I just forgot. I'm sorry."

Palryma realized that he had been too hasty and harsh with Bird. He stroked his feathers in consolation. "Ah.....never mind me Bird.....I'm just an anxious man in love....no fault or blame is yours.....I was over-excited with the expectation of a message from my love. Did you give her the tiny pearl from the shore-by-the sea? Does she look well? Is she safe?"

Bird raised his tiny head and nodded enthusiastically. "Yes...yes...and yes again Sir!" His whole tail was wiggling with excitement now. "I gave her the tiny pearl...and yes... she looks very well indeed and seems very safe." Palryma was thoroughly pleased with Bird's report.

Palryma placed a quick kiss on the top of Bird's head. "That's what Rosie did, Sir! She gave me a kiss and I asked her if I had to give the kiss to you along with the message!" Bird was wiggling his tail and flapping his wings in complete excitement now.

"What's this you say!!" said Palryma in mock horror "my love gave you a kiss!!? Bird was nodding his head and flapping his wings and wiggling his tail all at once. "Yes, Sir! And a very nice kiss it was!"

"Well, well well" said Palryma mocking himself in ponderment "whatever shall I think about all this kissing?"

"Rosie said I didn't have to kiss you, Sir......just give you the message! So maybe that's a little less kissing now!"

"Just let me think now a bit..." he answered continuing to play with the "seriousness" of his decision.

"It's quite a nice message, Sir.....I'd like to hurry up and give it to you!"

Finally Palryma broke into laughter and said "Oh...alright Bird! If you insist. Give me the message."

"Rosie told me that I was to whisper it into your ear, Sir!" With an expectant smile upon his handsome face, Palryma lowered his eyelids and raised Bird up to his ear. When Bird finished delivering the message, he lifted his eyelids and his violet eyes shone more brilliantly than they ever had in his whole entire life.

He moved Bird away from his ear so he could see his fine-feathered friend. "She said THAT about me!!! She actually said that to you about me!!"

"Yes Sir! Those are her words. That is her message exactly as she gave it to me" affirmed Bird.

"Sweet Lenora-ga! Are you certain Bird? You gave the message exactly, didn't you?"

"Yes Sir. Word for word. What does it mean, if I may ask?"

"SHE LOVES ME, BIRD!!! MY ALLURA ROSE LOVES ME!!"

Bird could barely contain himself. He was wiggling and flapping all over the place. "Oh...this is a happy day indeed, Sir! A very happy day."

It was then, at that very moment, that Palryma noticed the Cannerello Cupid flowers that encircled Dalo grave. He began to walk towards the grave with Bird still on his arm.

"What pretty flowers, Sir" remarked Bird as Palryma stood by the grave "I do not recall that they were here earlier today. Where did they come from?"

Palryma knew and he was flushed with love and pride for his guide. "They are from Dalo, Bird."

"How can that be, Sir? What exactly does it mean?"

"It means that Dalo is still with us. It means he understands what it means to be in love with the most beautiful girl you have ever seen. It means he is happy for me."

"Is he happy for Rosie too, Sir?'

"I would say that with these beautiful flowers here, Dalo is happiest of all for Rosie." He blew a kiss at the grave and turned to walk back to the cottage. "We should go back inside, Bird. I have more news to tell my parents."

"I have more news as well, Sir. I must tell you of my flight last night."

With his back now turned away from Dalo's grave, Palryma could not see that the Cannerello Cupid flowers disappeared from Dalo's grave just as sure as they had suddenly appeared.

It seemed on this day that all messages that needed to be delivered were, in fact, nicely delivered.

Chapter Twenty-Four

The new morning in Goosra had given Palryma's parents the night to sleep on the information from their son that he had been summoned to meet with Great Ben. Both were concerned about the nature of an audience with such an exhaulted legend. Everyone in the land knew about Great Ben. Stories about him were mythical and his abundant generosity touched many, many people. No one was certain of his age and it was, if truth be told, a matter of nothing more than simple curiosity among the villagers. What was important was that a meeting with Great Ben was no small matter. Simmee-Sammy. the village historian, would definitely have to record this in his Book of Events.

"Shall we give you something to present to Great Ben upon your meeting?" asked Merrilyee. "How will you get there?" asked his father "Are you certain of his location?"

Palryma thought the time was right to tell his parents about Sum-Timmy. "I have a new guide." he stated with some hesitation in his voice. "He presented himself to me when I returned from the shore-by-the-sea with Dalo's body."

"Then why is he not here to present himself as Dalo did?" questioned Bestra "It seems rather impolite of him not to do that."

"I am not quite sure of him myself, father. He said that

Batoowa sent him to me and that he was to be my new guide. I don't think I really have any further say in the matter." Bestra and Merrilyee looked at each other with deep concern. "I would feel more at ease, Palryma, if I could detect a bit more confidence in your voice." said his mother.

"Oh...I am certain that I will be fine. I told Sum-Timmy that Dalo would want me to trust him...so I will. I think there is no cause for concern."

"That's the problem we are having, son. All your life you have always thought that things will be fine. You have never bothered yourself with anything except the most positive points of life. I think it is the main reason why you were such a fearless hunter." Palryma brimmed with lovely reflections about his former life. "Yes, father....I was quite a good hunter, wasn't I?"

"But, your hunting days are over." quickly answered Bestra. "You are a chalice maker now. Will this man called Sum-Timmy be able to guide and protect you as Dalo did?"

"I have placed my faith in Batoowa, father. He chose me to become a chalice maker. I still don't know why, but I must abide by his choice...and he has chosen Sum-Timmy to be my new guide."

Bestra looked at Merrilyee and shrugged. "I still want to meet this Sum-Timmy fellow."

"I promise that I will bring him home after I have met with Great Ben. I must forewarn you though, he is every bit as strange looking as Dalo – but in a completely different way! Upon my return, we can all have a celebration of my marriage intentions!"

"Speaking of which" Merrilyee interjected with a mother's curiosity "I cannot imagine why a young woman would not want to marry such a wonderful young man as yourself,

Palryma. But, before you go making wedding plans and inviting friends to stand by your side, may I ask if you have actually made a formal request of marriage to Allura Rose that she can consider properly? It seems almost impolite not to have done that."

Palryma was almost shamed by his mother's question. "Well...not an actual formal one...but I love her truly and I know that she loves me...I have a message from her that Bird delivered to me just last night and I am certain now that we will marry!"

"That settles it!" cried Bestra with the kind of declaration only a father can give "your mother is right! There will be no more talk of wedding intentions until you assure us that you have made a formal request to your beloved and she has answered "Yes". That is the decision of Bestra, your father — not Batoowa — and you must abide by it. Chalice Maker or not, we are still your parents and you cannot shame this house with impoliteness."

There was barely a moment of silence before Palryma rose to his feet and clapped his hands together in great enthusiasm.

"Done!!!" he said with a bow "I will abide by your decision and make a formal request to my love as soon as I return from my audience with Great Ben. I have no doubt that she will accept and I will bring her here to meet you! In fact, when I am with Great Ben, I will ask him to preside over the ceremony. He is a chalice maker and I think he will most likely be very happy to honor a request such as that from another chalice maker, don't you think?! We will have a grand celebration and it will be a great day in Goosra when everyone meets my beautiful Allura Rose!" Bestra and Merrilyee looked at each other in their moment of silence.

"Now, I must collect Bird and we have to start on our journey. I am to meet Sum-Timmy at the edge of the wet fields without delay."

Bestra looked at his own beautiful beloved wife of 24 years. "Did you teach him that level of confidence when I was not looking, my love?"

"I think, dear husband that when it comes to marrying the girl he loves the best, our son inherited that level of confidence from you!"

"Perhaps..." Bestra replied with a bit of red in his cheeks "and it will serve him well in marriage. Of this I am certain. I look forward to meeting this forest girl, Allura Rose."

Chapter Twenty-Five

Before Palryma and Bird left the village of Goosra entirely, they stopped quickly at the bakery of Bethnee and Beeloma for a few sweet couldas. Beeloma had just finished a batch when the adventuresome two-some walked in. "Hello and heavens above, Palryma." said Beeloma with a fresh tray of Palryma's favorite bakery treat in his hands. "It seems you are right on time for a new batch of sweet couldas. How would you agree with me on that?"

Palryma exaggerated his whiffing of the familiar aroma that drew him to the bakery since he was a boy. "Hello and heavens above to you Beeloma. When it comes to freshly baked sweet couldas, I'm afraid that I will always and forever have to agree with you in any way possible!!"

"Well, Bethnee and I have already heard the news that you have a very important appointment to meet with Great Ben so we rose with the first rays of the morning sun and started to bake some of your favorite treats to sustain you on your journey. My wife knew for certain that you would stop by on your way out of the village."

"You know me very well my friend...very, very well. When have I ever NOT stopped here on my way in or out of Goosra? This bakery is like a second home to me filled with grand memories."

Beeloma set the tray of goodies on the table. "And I see you have a traveling companion as well. Good Morning to you Bird! I trust you are enjoying Goosra. I hope you like sweet couldas!"

"Oh yes, indeed" replied Bird "Oh, like them very well indeed. Almost better than too-too-too berries from the forest! Why, when I was dying and Palryma took care to save me...it was sweet couldas that he fed me....they brought me back to life! Oh yes, indeed...I truly love sweet couldas!"

"Wonderful — just wonderful to hear! I'll put a few extra in this sack — enough to take you through your journey and back home again."

With an explanation that they must be quick afoot in order to meet up with Sum-Timmy, Palryma gave extra special thanks to his baker friend and made haste for the dirt road leading out of the village.

"Safe journey to you chalice maker.....safe journey. Come back to us soon. Come back safe and sound." Beeloma said as he watched Palryma, with Bird perched on his shoulder, walk away in the distance.

As they made way towards the edge of the wet fields, Palryma absent-mindedly began whistling his favorite walking song "One Love for Me".

"Sir, isn't that Rosie's song you are whistling?"

"It wasn't when I first started whistling it a long time ago, Bird. But it surely is now! Why don't you chirp along with me? We will surely miss Dalo's thumping along with his fat feet and wiggly toes, but why don't we whistle and chirp together?"

"Oh, I surely do like Rosie, Sir! I will do my best chirping on this song!" And so they did....the chalice maker and his bird.....chirping in perfect harmony to the newly christened "Rosie's Song." Their harmonious rendition was loud enough to be heard in the forest and caused an unusual stirring that Palryma noticed down the road somewhat as they neared their agreed meeting spot with Sum-Timmy.

Palryma pointed it out to Bird who concurred that something or someone was rustling about in the low-lying bluebell bushes just ahead. It was obvious from the way the delicate bluebell flowers were swaying from side to side. "I wonder what it is, Sir. Is it Sum-Timmy trying to play tricks on us?"

Palryma did not think that this was any kind of trick and cautioned that they approach this mysterious moving object very carefully. "The forest in Goosra, especially the part close to the wet fields, have always carried many hidden surprises." he said to Bird. They stayed on the far side of the dirt road and were dumbstruck by what they saw as they edged closer and closer.

"Is that a horse I see!? A horse lying on its side in the bluebell bushes?" asked Palryma with more than just a hint of the incredulous in his voice. Bird did not respond immediately. He wanted to be certain of what he, himself, saw struggling to survive.

"It IS a horse, Sir!! I think it must be one of the dark-as-night flying Reelatta horses that tried to chase me from the sky on my flight to Goosra. As I told you, I saw two of them drop from the sky as I escaped their rath and flew away. This must be one of them!" Palryma inched ever so slowly towards what both he and Bird now recognized as a fallen horse — a fallen and clearly wounded dark-as-night flying Reelatta horse. "Sir, please be careful. Don't get too close. These horses must have orders to kill from Hurrah III. They have evil execution in their hearts."

Palryma stopped moving and peered ominously at the animal. "Something is amiss here, Bird." He stepped a bit closer. What he noticed gave him great concern. "This is not a full-grown horse at all. Did you not tell me that three horses tried to chase you out of the sky?" Bird nodded. "Are you certain that all three were full grown horses?"

"The two who were closest to me most definitely were full-grown and full of hate as well." remembered Bird.

"But what about the third one? Was he close to you as well?"

"Come to think of it now, Sir....the third horse was somewhat in the distance from the other two.....almost as though he was struggling to keep up. I just assumed that he was also a full-grown horse and appeared to be so in the distance."

"Surely you must know by now that things are not always as they appear in this land, Bird." Palryma said matter-of-factly.

He crossed the dirt road and stepped into the forest, closer to the bluebell bushes. He was now only a few feet from the animal and concluded that it, indeed, was most certainly not a full-grown horse, but neither was it a pony. It was definitely a dark-as-night flying Reelatta horse......but a young one who seemed to have broken its right front leg. The rustling of the bluebell bushes was cause by the young horse's repeated, but failed, attempts to rise on its three remaining good legs. The young horse had a frightened look in its tired eyes.

"If you have any arrows with you, please kill me." said the young horse with uncompromising sadness. "I am done for anyway." Palryma was aghast that anything so young, animal or not, would beg to be killed. His heart immediately went out to the suffering horse.

"I do not have any arrows, so I cannot kill you, as you request, young horse. But even if I did still have my arrows, I would never shoot them through an animal whose request is as repugnant as yours! Why do you want to die?!"

"I cannot get up, I cannot fly, I am lost and I dare not go back to the Castle of Hurrah III." Tears began to stream from the eyes of the young horse. "It is over for me."

Bird did not wait for Palryma to answer. He spoke immediately. "Young horse, were you in the sky with two others two days ago? Did you try to kill me? Did you try to do this upon the command of Hurrah III? I believe I saw you in the sky at a distance. We mean you no harm, but I believe it might have been you. Am I correct?"

The young horse closed his eyes in shame. "I did not know of any "killing mission". On my honor I tell you this as I lay here dying. I was only told that I must follow the two older horses. It was quite difficult for me to keep up, as they were bigger and stronger than I. I had to do as I was told or be whipped again. The horses dare not question a command from Hurrah III. You have no idea of his rath. It is like a thousand angry gods and if I go back to the castle, he will surely kill me himself" he sobbed. "I just want to go back to my family but I am so lost I don't know what to do. I'll never get back now. I can neither walk nor fly so, please, just kill me right here and now. Spare me any more misery."

Palryma knelt next to the young horse and tried to comfort him. Bird quietly told him who he used to be. "He changed my beautiful white feathers to yellow. He convinced me that yellow was the color of wisdom and I foolishly believed him. He renamed me Settela and believe me when I tell you, young horse, I know full well the rath of Hurrah III. I carry a reminder of it with me every day. See here...when he threw me out of the castle window with such force, he ripped my claw off! Oh for certain....I think you can tell me no new tales about the rath of that wretched man."

"Leave me here. I just want to die." cried the young horse.

"Are you absolutely certain that is exactly what you want to do?" said a voice that was neither Palryma's nor Bird's. "For as certain as you lay amongst the bluebell bushes, if you die, you will not see your family again. So...I'll ask you again, young horse...are you absolutely certain that you want to die?"

It was Sum-Timmy. He simply appeared without announcement or warning from the low-lying bluebell bushes. Palryma fell back on his haunches and said "Hello and heavens above, Sum-Timmy. I did not see you there!"

"Of course you did not, Mr. Palryma. For the moment I was not meant to be seen. For the moment, I wanted to see if you and Bird would show the young horse, here, some compassion and I am happy to see that you have done just fine."

"Where were you?" asked Bird. Sum-Timmy replied that he was in the bushes. "Well...to be more exact – I was one of the bushes and now I am not!! That's the kind of guide I am! Everywhere and nowhere at the same time. You'll get used to it." Palryma and Bird shook their heads in complete wonderment and confusion.

"But, this situation is not about me at all." declared Sum-Timmy "it is about our new friend here, Young Horse." Bird and Palryma nodded in agreement and looked at the animal on the ground who Sum-Timmy had obviously just named Young Horse.

"So what it is going to be Young Horse? Do you truly desire death?" No one moved. For a moment no one spoke. Young Horse's eyes welled with streaming tears as he laid his head back on the ground. "Please help me...please...if you can... help me."

"Much better!!" shouted Sum-Timmy "Very much better....

its always much better to ask for help than to give up and die!! How would you agree with me on that, Mr. Palryma?"

Bird nodded his head enthusiastically and flapped his wings as Palryma responded. "Why, of course, Sum-Timmy — I would have to agree with you in every way possible!" He tried to dry the flowing tears from Young Horse's face. "It is always much better to keep on struggling....to try and carry on rather than try and end your life! Why, it's true that's a very easy choice! Keep living! You have made the right choice Young Horse! Bird and I will help you...and Sum-Timmy will help you as well, won't you Sum-Timmy?"

"I am your guide, Mr. Palryma. I will gladly do as you ask. But Young Horse must be willing to help himself, as well. That is the real key to living."

"Where do I start? What shall I do?" whispered Young Horse.

Palryma and Bird had a brief, private discussion and then told Young Horse that it would be best if he tried very hard to get up on his three legs. "We will help you up," confirmed Palryma. "I am quite strong and I can push you up from behind. Don't worry, we can do this together."

"And I will shout great encouragement to you, as I am too small to help lift you, Young Horse, but I will be cheering you on!"

With that, Young Horse began the struggle to get to his feet. It was not easy, but without the help of Palryma and Bird, it would have been impossible.

"This is a very, very good beginning." said Sum-Timmy "in point of fact, it is quite a memorable one. We are on our way! Great Ben will be pleased."

Chapter Twenty-Six

It was a struggle, no doubt, but the end result was that Young Horse was finally on his legs. Well, more correctly, he was on three legs as the fourth, the front right leg, was shattered and of no useful support. The strain of rising up and the attendant pain was obvious on Young Horse's face. Bird's cheering and Palryma's muscles had a great deal to do with the fact that Young Horse was no longer lying in the bluebell bushes. Sum-Timmy watched him rise without saying a word. He observed as he always did, and did so with a silent knowing that marked his character as Palryma's new guide. Sum-Timmy made it plain that he knew what he knew and nothing more. What was not plain was just how much the new guide actually knew.

Palryma stood very close to the horse's broken leg and lent support where Young Horse, himself, could provide none. Bird was perched atop Young Horse's head, in between his ears, and continued to congratulate him on the successful rise. "We all knew you could do it, Young Horse....we believed in you and see what happened? You are better off than you were a few minutes ago....and better still...you are not dead!"

It was obvious that it was difficult for Young Horse to lift his head completely and his posture still reflected a sadness that did not go away with his rising up. "But, now what?" he asked "I am up, to be sure, even if it is only on three legs. But I cannot run or walk. Am I to stay standing in these bushes forever?" Palryma stroked his long, silky mane and did not respond. It was time for Sum-Timmy to talk.

"Not unless you want to." said the guide

"Please, please" replied the horse in between winces of pain "no more puzzles. I have risen as you asked but I do not know where to go from here."

"Where do you want to be?" was Sum-Timmy's answer.

Young Horse began to cry again. "With my family....I want to be back with my family. I miss them so."

"Hmmm....yes, of course. I see. It is natural to want to be with your family. I see your point. And that could eventually happen....it surely could, but I do not see how that can happen right now."

Palryma could not bear to see Young Horse crying again and said "Sum-Timmy! If you can help him why don't you? Can't you see that he is in pain?"

"But, Mr. Palryma, I am trying to help. I must hear Young Horse tell me where he wants to be."

"He told you!" said Palryma sharply "he wants to be with his family."

Sum-Timmy stepped back a bit for composure's sake. "Mr. Palryma, I heard that. But that is where he wants to be in the future. I want him to tell me where he wants to be right now!"

Sum-Timmy looked at Young Horse and repeated himself. "Do you understand what I am saying? Tell me where you want to be right here and now."

It was clear to both Bird and Palryma that Young Horse was getting weaker as the pain in his broken leg grew stronger. They were stymied as to how they could help.

Finally, Young Horse collected himself enough to make an answer. "Right now...right here and now...I want to be standing on all four legs....I want to be standing here with none of them broken or shattered. That is what I want. That is where I want to be."

"Beautiful!!" shouted Sum-Timmy "that is excellent. Now I can help you. Now I know what you want!"

With no more than that to say, Sum-Timmy's stick-like figure transformed itself into the thin outline of a huge box shaped window right before everyone's eyes. Whether he was alerted or alarmed, Bird immediately flew from atop Young Horse's head to perch himself in the protectorate of Palryma's shoulder. Palryma peered curiously at the strange looking window frame positioned directly in front of Young Horse. All three of them waited breathlessly for some explanation or direction.

"Walk through, Young Horse." was all they heard. Still, Young Horse did not move.

"Go on, now....step through the window. Have faith and you will get to where you want to be. Step through."

"Step through to where?" quivered Young Horse.

"Why...to where you want to be, of course! Standing here in the bluebell bushes with four good legs! Come now....step through the window. Mr. Palryma...Bird...if you would step back a few places, if you please." Palryma complied and nervously waited for Young Horse to make a move. "Come on, Young Horse. You can do this!" said Bird with a quiet cheer.

With all the strength and faith that he possessed, Young Horse began to limp through the window frame. First, his head and neck. Then his front left leg was through. The push from his hindquarters and back legs propelled him all the way through and as soon as he was clear, the window frame disappeared.

"Sweet Lenora-ga, I do not believe what I see!" shouted Palryma. "Bird, do you see what I see?!" Bird was flapping and nodding and wiggling so much that he fell off Palryma's shoulder. When Palryma picked him up, he shouted "Sir!! Sum-Timmy is quite a good guide, isn't he?"

Sum-Timmy, now restored to his own remarkable-looking stick-frame, was standing at the side of the road. "It was not really me, Bird. It really was all about Young Horse. He knew where he wanted to be and he believed he could get there. All I did was provide him with an opportunity. It was his decision to use it......and, as always, a little help and encouragement from his friends did not hurt!"

Young Horse had yet to speak and was standing very, very still....stunned by what just happened. He wondered if he was dreaming, but a side glance showed him that Palryma and Bird were right there - just as they had been a few moments ago when he was in terrible pain from his broken leg. But now there was no broken leg. There was no hint of him ever having had a broken leg. There was no scar. It was as if his fall from the sky had never happened.

Right now...right here and now, he was exactly where he told Sum-Timmy he wanted to be....standing in the bluebell bushes without a broken leg!

The miracle of his own faith began to overcome him and he started to prance and dance like a young pony. He trotted and ran and kicked up and down the dirt road. He rose on his back legs and let out a whinney that he wanted his far-away family to hear. "I am well!!! I am well!! I am well!" he cried. "Look at me! I am well!" His happiness was a thing to behold.

He galloped down the road and back again. He came to

a full halt right before Sum-Timmy and bowed gracefully. "I am in your debt. I do not know how to repay you. You gave my life back to me." he said ever most sincerely. "I am whole again."

"All I did was guide you, Young Horse. You did the rest yourself....with the help of your friends over there, of course!"

Young Horse walked over to Palryma and nuzzled him with his big head. Palryma responded with a hug as best he could manage around a horse. Bird jumped back onto Young Horse's head. "I like the view from here!" he chirped.

"I will never forget you M'Lord. You have a kindness in your heart the likes of which I have not seen since my father showed me how to fly when I was but a small, young pony. I thought such kindness had disappeared from my life forever when I was kidnapped and brought to the Castle of Hurrah III."

Palryma, but not Sum-Timmy, was shocked at this news. "You were kidnapped?" he said.

Young Horse nodded. "And blindfolded, too. All the dark-as-night flying Reelatta horses are kidnapped, blindfolded and brought to the castle to do the bidding of Hurrah III. We are all then painted black and most always are ordered, from that time on, to fly only at night."

Young Horse explained that the kidnappings had been going on since the early years of Hurrah's reign. All the horses were from a pastoral land, rich in heavy black soil and thick forests, called Mora-Mora-Na. It was on the very furthest edge of Latima. It was a land unspoiled by anything, except kidnappings. Palryma stated that he had never heard of Mora-Mora-Na. "Although, I cannot say that I am surprised," he added "we never go to Latima much less any land that is on its far reaches."

"Is your family still there?" asked Bird.

"I suspect so. I surely hope so....that is, if they have not been kidnapped. I surely do long to return to see them again but as I told you before, broken leg or not, I am very lost. I don't think I know my way back home."

Then Bird had what he thought was an excellent idea. "Sir! I'll bet Great Ben would be able to tell Young Horse the right way home, don't you think?"

Palryma shrugged and looked towards his guide. "Sum-Timmy?"

"We will never know, Mr. Palryma until we get there. And we will never get there by standing here on the dirt road next to the Wet Fields."

"Is it far?" asked Palryma "I am sure Young Horse can make the walk now that he has four good legs again."

"I don't see why not. They look as good as new!" declared Sum-Timmy.

Then Young Horse had what he thought was an excellent idea. "But, M'Lord...why must we walk? I can fly you there with ease. Bird can stay right where he is in between my ears and you can jump on my back with Sum-Timmy and I can fly us all to where you need to go. It is the very least that I can do."

Palryma looked at his guide once again. "If we fly, Sum-Timmy, we are certain to be at Great Ben's before dark, wouldn't you say?" Sum-Timmy only nodded and said "If you wish it to be so, Mr. Palryma...it will be so!"

"Ahhhhh...." added Bird with a soulful sigh "Home before dark! It's always best to be home before dark!"

And off they went. Bird in between Young Horse's ears and both Palryma and Sum-Timmy astride his back. The four of them went flying away to make the appointment with Great Ben.

Chapter Twenty-Seven

High in the sky and free as....well....free as birds and horses – and chalice makers and guides, of course! Young Horse was flying steady and strong. His wings never tired and his eyes were clearly on the horizon. Bird was in heaven. "This is the nicest flight I have ever made, Sir! And I'm not working a bit! It is lovely to see all this beautiful land from above and not have to worry if I will get tired."

"Speaking of which" Palryma chimed in "are you feeling alright Young Horse? Tell us if you begin to tire and we can stop for a rest."

"No, M'Lord" added Young Horse quickly "I feel wonderful. It's no bother at all having passengers. It's quite nice, in fact! Have we a long way to go yet?"

Sum-Timmy explained that their arrival at Great Ben's was imminent. There was a low-lying ridge in the distance and beyond that was a great lake. At the far edge of the great lake, atop an over looking bluff, was the home of Great Ben. "We will be there shortly, Mr. Palryma. I remind you that we would still be walking on the long dirt road past the wet fields if it were not for the generosity of Young Horse. He has made a long journey into an easy flight. Great Ben will be pleased with him."

The wings of Young Horse continued to take the Chalice

Maker and his friends closer to their destination. "I am really looking forward to this." said Palryma "I have so much I want to ask Great Ben."

"He will have the answers." replied Sum-Timmy.

"You don't think he will be upset because I have brought Bird and Young Horse along, do you?"

"Not at all, Mr. Palryma! I am quite sure he knows about it already."

For all the time it took to fly over the great lake, no one spoke a word. Palryma was not certain if it was because the beauty of the lake was making them speechless or because with every flap of Young Horse's wings, they were that much closer to meeting Great Ben. No matter what it was, a proper, unspoken solemnity caused their conversations to cease.

Bird was the first to break the silence. "I see it, Sir! I see the bluff at the edge of this great lake and there is a very big house atop the bluff!" An airy feeling inside Palryma's stomach suddenly disappeared as he realized that soon they would arrive.

"We are arriving, Mr. Palryma." announced Sum-Timmy. "Young Horse, fly over the house and set us down on the back grounds. There is more than enough room for us to land there."

With a few more powerful flaps of his wings, Young Horse followed Sum-Timmy's direction and then began to glide easily over the top of the house. His sturdy eye saw that he could lower himself and his passengers safely onto a very large area covered with soft blue and green grass.

"Well done, Young Horse!! Very well done!" exclaimed Sum-Timmy. "You have delivered us safely here and I am most thankful."

"Yes. Thank you very much, Young Horse." added Palryma as he stepped onto the grass. "Flying with you was an adventure all by itself!" Bird, saying nothing, gave Young Horse's ear a tiny peck with his beak before he jumped onto Palryma's shoulder.

"With pleasure M'Lord. I would do it again for you at any time."

Palryma looked around at the vast expanse of land behind him. It was a remarkable landscape repleat with streams and brooks and magnificent trees on every slope. It was a marked difference to the serenity posed by the great lake they had just flown over before touching down on the bluff. Great Ben's house, which resembled a type of castle more than it did a house – certainly larger than any cottage he ever saw in Goosra – was formidable but, strangely, not imposing. Large stones with multi-colored specs that composed the fortress-like back curvature of the abode were covered in spots and spaces by a blue green moss that matched the grass upon which Palryma stood. The windowpanes appeared to have faces in them or at least paintings of faces in them from one glance —- and then no faces or painting of faces in them at all from another glance. It was quite befuddling.

There was a huge chimneystack on each side of the house and the aromatic scent of a burning wood fire was easy to detect. What was odd was that out of one chimney stack came a magnificent rose, almost red, colored smoke and out of the other chimney stack rose a bright blue colored smoke. They mingled in the air above the castle-like house and made a beautiful violet colored smoke – the color of Palryma's eyes. It was seeing this violet smoke that Palryma remembered for the first time some part of his initiation rite as a chalice maker. "I remember being clouded and surrounded by violet smoke." he whispered to himself. "It's funny that I have not thought much about the initiation rite at all since it happened. So much has happened since that day and it seems so very long ago." he mused.

"Sir, what shall we do now that we are here?" asked Bird. Palryma did not have time to answer before another's reply was heard.

"You shall come inside. You are all my guests and you can rest here. I invite you."

It was Great Ben. He was standing at the window frame where the glass pane, present just a few moments ago, had now disappeared. He motioned with his hand and beckoned the travelers to enter.

The young chalice maker from Goosra looked with his mouth agape at the reknown, legendary chalice maker from thousands of years gone by. Two different chalice makers beholding each other for the first time. Great Ben smiled but Palryma's mouth stayed agape. It seemed impossible for him to close his jaw.

"Perhaps I should speak first." said Great Ben in a voice so smooth and pleasing that it took your breath away to hear it. He seemed aware of the lock on Palryma's jaw.

"Well then.....as you say in Goosra — Hello and heavens above! That is what you say, isn't it?" Palryma nodded repeatedly but could manage no words.

"It is of course!! That is exactly what we say!" burst Bird trying to rescue Palryma from an embarrassing lack of response. "That's what we say allright — Hello and heavens above!"

"So?" questioned Great Ben, clearly waiting to be greeted.

"Oh....Oh...I see" said Bird, feigning confidence "Hello and heavens above! What a nice place you have here! How would you agree with me on that?"

"Yes. Hello to you and your heavens, kind sir. Surely you must already know that you have a nice place!" added Young

Horse, trying to help Bird and Palryma. But he was not from Goosra so he was not used to speaking the honored and time-worn village greeting.

Great Ben smiled wryly at his guests. "It's home" he said with some air of depreciation. "A lot of people like to think of it as home while they are here. I hope you will do the same. Please come in."

Palryma began to edge forward with Bird on his shoulder. Young Horse stared strangely at the doorway. "Ummmm... kind sir....it does not look to me as though I will be able to fit through the door....with my wings and all, you see." Great Ben placed his hands on his hips and began to laugh. "Well, Nee-rahma.....why don't you do exactly what you did in the forest? Just as Sum-Timmy bade you to do. Just as before, you only have to step through. You are welcome here."

No one had called Young Horse "Nee-rahma" since the day he was kidnapped from his home and brought to the Castle of Hurrah III. It stunned Young Horse to hear it. The memories of his former life had almost been whipped out of him and he felt a strange unease at the sound of the name his parents gave him: "Nee-rahma".

"How did you know my name, kind sir? I am ashamed to say that I had almost forgotten it. No one has called me Nee-rahma in a very long time."

"I know everything about you Nee-rahma." replied Great Ben. "Now won't you all come inside? You have traveled far to come see me and I thought I would offer you a splendid meal to mark your arrival."

Palryma motioned for Young Horse to lead the way. He and Bird followed.

And all three of them simply stepped through the door-way into the home of Great Ben.

Chapter Twenty-Eight

Cavernous would have been a good word to describe the room they all walked into. Surprisingly cavernous – for it did not appear to be that way from the outside. But there was closeness – a welcoming intimacy to the room that matched Great Ben's warm beckon that they all enter. It was homey – huge, but very, very homey. There was a massive table in the center of the room and a roaring fire in the fireplace that was equal in size to any fire that Palryma's father, Bestra, ever lit in the back of his cottage in Goosra.

"It's a much larger room than one might think from standing outside your fine home." said Palryma, finally finding his voice.

"Ah.....well, young chalice maker not everything is as it appears to be all the time now, is it?" answered Great Ben. "Take me, for example."

Palryma nodded in deference. "Please excuse my earlier silence outside. I did not greet you properly but I was quite overwhelmed....awed, in fact, to be in your presence. You are a legend and I have never been face to face with a legend before."

"I am a chalice maker. You are a chalice maker. Nothing more. Legend has nothing to do with it."

"But you are known throughout the land and..."

Great Ben interrupted him. "And soon enough....in time....

you, too, will be known throughout the land. ....including where I live right here in Matra-Matoo."

"Oh, is that the name of the place where we are now?" chirped Bird "I think I have never seen such a beautiful place. How do you greet people here?"

"We say 'hi' said the master. "For example, when I see you tomorrow morning, I will say "Hi Bird" and you will respond by saying "Hi Great Ben". Its very simple. We like to keep things very simple here in Matra-Matoo."

"Is that how we shall address you, kind sir?.....we can call you 'Great Ben'?

"Of course....of course!!! That's what you must do. I insist. And I shall call you Nee-rahma.......unless, of course, you prefer something else." Young Horse did not know what to say. His given name did not sound familiar to him anymore and it had a far away lonesome ring to his ears.

"Well you can call me Bird, Great Ben!!" "That's not my real name, but I don't like my real name anyway. I like my new name and my new life. So...Bird it is!"

Great Ben said he knew all about Bird's old name and all about his old life. "You are very lucky to have been rescued by my fellow chalice maker here. I hope you know just how lucky."

"Bird has been a good friend to me, Great Ben. I feel like I am the lucky one to have him in my life now.....and Young Horse, too! They are very special to me." announced Palryma with great pride in his friends. "And Sum-Timmy, too....wherever he is!"

Great Ben explained that Sum-Timmy was inside the house but oftentimes just like to fade into the walls. "He's here....probably just taking a rest.....speaking of which, please have a seat at the table. The feast awaits us."

When Palryma looked at the table, it seemed as though

he was home in Goosra. There was a platter of roast Simeeore boar, pig-nitty soup and two big plates filled with sweet coul-das and toody bread with white frosting. There was a bowl of too-too-too berries for Bird and a pile of hay mixed with mealy-more and crushed sugar surrounded by carrots and apples for Young Horse.

"How beautiful!" cried Palryma "and I have just the stom-ach for this! How did you gather it all?"

"Oh....I just thought you all might be hungry by the time you arrived and so I thought up the meal....just thought was all it took and there it was! Please, everyone help yourselves!" invited Great Ben.

Palryma was not sure what Great Ben meant by that but, for the moment, he was too hungry to reflect upon it. He began to devour the Simeeore boar. Bird was so happy that he began to chirp and whistle in between gulping down the red and blue too-too-too berries. "I never saw blue colored berries before Great Ben. They are delicious!"

Great Ben took delight in watching his guests eat their fill. "The red ones are from Goosra, Bird, and the blue ones are from right here in Matra-Matoo. I thought you might like to sample them both."

While Palryma was waiting for his pig-nitty soup to cool he looked around the room. It was hard not to notice the elegant chalices that sat atop the mantelpiece. They were every bit as gorgeous as legend had them to be. Palryma pointed to them and asked if they were Great Ben's handiwork. The mas-ter nodded. "I make a lot of chalices. Those above the fire are some of the early ones. They are all over the house. When you finish eating I will show you some more."

"I would like that very much, thank you." said Palryma. He hesitated for a moment and then added "Great Ben...not to be impolite or anything....but I must say that your....well.....

your looks.....they seem to be changing all the time....you know, right before us."

"I was wondering when you were going to notice!" Great Ben replied.

"Is that how everyone in Matra-Matoo appears?.....one look followed by another" asked Palryma.

Great Ben shook his head. "Nope. Just me!"

"And why is that?" said the young chalice maker with his typical curiosity.

"Because I am the face of every kind and loving soul you know of. I am the visual manifestation of the kindness you think of....the people whose generosity and love you admire. Sometimes I can appear to be a combination of two or three people all at once. It all depends on what you are thinking. So, you see...it pays to think good thoughts and to think about good people. It is what you will see in me. Nothing else is truly important."

"And......" added the master "I make a really nice chalice, too!"

Young Horse shook his silky mane and whinnied in approval. "Very good, Great Ben. I myself was just thinking of a kindness paid to me recently and when I looked at you, I saw that you resembled Palryma."

"My point exactly, Nee-rahma! Now you have it! Palryma paid you a fine kindness on the roadside next to the wet fields and it touched your heart. I am the visual aid, so to speak, that accompanies that thought."

"I see my father in you." said Palryma.

"As well you should" said Great Ben "for he is a kind and thoughtful man who loves your mother dearly."

"I thought I saw Dalo for a moment, but I said nothing – thinking that I was eating the too-too-too berries too fast!" cried Bird. "But now I think that I really did see him in you."

"No doubt, Bird. No doubt at all." said Great Ben "Dalo was also a very, very kind and thoughtful man."

"And the faces that I saw in the windows when we first arrived?" queried Palryma "they were there and then they were not? What about them?"

"Well, Palryma as with many things in life – it all depends upon how you look at it. You look one way and the faces are in the windows and you look another way and they are gone. I have had many, many visitors over the years here in Matro-Matoo. Some stay and some go. I leave it up to them. So, even when I, myself, look at the windows, the faces seem always to be changing. I just try to let everyone know that they are always welcome here. What they ultimately choose to do is never my decision.

When the feasting was done, Great Ben asked Palryma to come with him on a walk through the house. "I hope your friends will excuse us." he said. "Nee-rahma....if you and Bird would like to go back outside, please feel free. The evening air is something altogether wonderful in Matra-Matoo and the sky at this time is a color I am certain you have never seen before."

"I think I would like to lie in that beautiful blue and green grass that is outside!" replied Young Horse. "Come, Bird....rest between my ears. We can enjoy it together."

"Walk with me awhile, Palryma" said Great Ben. "There are some things I want to show you...some things I want to tell you."

And the two chalice makers went off into the remainder of the house.

Chapter Twenty-Nine

The morning sun in Matra-Matoo was unlike a morning sun anywhere in the land. It was as colorful as you wanted it to be...or it was just a single shade of your favorite hue. It all depended on who was looking at it. Its rays were visible and when touched, wrapped your hands in a tender, beguiling well of coolness. Warm sun, cool rays and an endless sky filled with birds of every breed and color who hummed, sang, chirped and danced with the clouds. Morning was a fine thing to wake up to in Matra-Matoo.

It was to this special glory of the day that Young Horse awoke. He was standing on all four legs before his eyes opened clearly enough to notice that all the black paint, savagely poured on his coat by wailing servants of Hurrah III, was completely gone. In its place was the coat he was born with..... soft golden in color with spots of white on his hindquarters and stomach. There was a spot of white on his forehead in the shape of a star. It was the shaking of his long silky white mane that caused Bird to waken suddenly from his resting place in between Young Horse' ears.

"Hi Nee-rahma. Hi Bird. I hope you had a fine, restful sleep under the stars." said Great Ben. He was leaning against the rock fence that separated him from a deep drop off the bluff on which his house sat.

Bird flew over to sit on a rock next to where Great Ben was leaning. "Hi Great Ben." He pointed to Young Horse with one of his wings. "Look at that! Young Horse looks like a new horse! What happened to him?" Great Ben picked Bird up off the rock and rested him in the cup of his two hands. "He now looks like his old self, Bird! And quite fine he looks, indeed." Bird nodded in agreement. "If Nee-rahma is meant to find his family again, as he wishes, it's best that they will be able to recognize him when they finally see him, don't you think?"

Young horse was turning in circles trying to get a full look at himself. "This is my coat....this is what......This is the coat I was born with! I remember it now! This is how I used to look!"

"And the star on your forehead?....do you recall its significance?" asked Great Ben.

Young Horse admitted that he could not.

"You are named after the beautiful star on your forehead." Great Ben explained "Nee-rahma means beautiful star."

"You do look very beautiful Young Horse." said Bird admiringly. "Especially now that all the paint is gone!"

"I think I remember some bits of it now." said an exhaulted Young Horse "I think I remember some people...maybe friends...admiring the star on my forehead. I think they said it made me special.....but I haven't felt very special in a long time."

"It's because you were held captive.....kept away from who you really were. No one can feel special when they are held against their will and forced to be something other than what they really are. No one is free if they are painted up in order to be something they are not. You are free now, Nee-rahma.... now you can choose what you want to be." declared Great Ben. "Here in Matra-Matoo everyone is free to be whatever and whoever they were born to be."

Young Horse walked silently over to the master and gave him a big, warm nuzzle. "Thank you, Great Ben. Thank you forever and ever and ever." Great Ben moved his lips closer to Nee-rahma's ears and whispered "You *will* be united with your family once again.....in time you will all be reunited. Have faith in this for by the grace of Sweet Lenora-ga, I tell you it is true."

"And just what is going on here, I ask?" jested Palryma as he walked across the blue and green grass towards his friends.

"Hi Palryma."

"Hi Sir!!!"

"Hi M'Lord!"

"That is a fine trio of Matra-Matoo greetings! How would you agree with me on that, Great Ben?"

"In every way possible, my fellow chalice maker. In every way possible!"

"Spoken like a true Goosra-ian!" laughed the young chalice maker.

"But we are in Matro-Matoo, Sir! Look what happened to Young Horse overnight here in Matra-Matoo!" Bird cried.

"Where is Sum-Timmy?" asked Palryma.

"He has decided to stay here in Matra-Matoo for a few extra days. He will meet you back at the cave. Not to worry." replied Great Ben.

Palryma draped one arm over the low part of Young Horse's neck and began to rub the front part of his neck with the other. "I must say, Young Horse, the night air in Matra-Matoo seems to have agreed with you. You look quite well!"

"I have become my old self, M'Lord — perhaps you did not recognize me!"

"Then you must be Nee-rahma now. I think that is what I should probably call you....and by the way, I think you should call me Palryma."

Young Horse gave his mane a good shake. "Oh, I don't know about that M'Lord! I don't think I can take all these name changes all at once."

"Everyone can still call me Bird!" shouted Bird with glee "I will always be Bird!"

"You are a rare one, indeed, Bird!" said Great Ben with a great smile "You are a rare bird, that's for certain."

"And do you know what else, Sir?" Bird said excitedly "if Dalo was here, I know exactly what he would call Young Horse!"

"And what is that my friend?" teased Palryma.

"Well, Sir...Dalo always called you 'Pallie'. And he called Allura Rose 'Rosie'. He would call Young Horse 'Youngie'.... he surely would...no doubt of it!"

Young Horse whinnied in delight. "That is the best, Bird! I think that I like 'Youngie' the best for now.....if that meets with your approval Great Ben."

"This is Matra-Matoo.....it will be as *you* wish!"

"Then 'Youngie' it is!....for now!" declared Young Horse.

"Fine and settled then" stated Palryma "we must be on our way now."

Bird and Youngie seemed almost sad at Palryma's announcement. Matra-Matoo had become very comfortable to both of them in a very short time. But Bird knew they had business back in Goosra and so he hopped from the warm cup of Great Ben's hands up to his now familiar resting spot in between Youngie's ears. "I am ready when you are, Sir."

"I was honored to have you and your wonderful friends come visit me" said Great Ben to Palryma. "You must take it to heart when I tell you that it was a pleasure meeting you. I hope you will see your way sometime in the future to come back to Matra-Matoo and visit me again. I will always be thinking of you....always. Never forget that."

Palryma was stunned again by the masters spirit of warmth and generosity. "Great Ben...it is I who was honored to be here. I will keep your friendship in my heart always."

"And you will remember all the things we spoke of late into the night?"

"Always" answered Palryma.

"And even all the things that you cannot see right away.... you will do what?"

Palryma smiled at the test. "I will be patient for their arrival for I know now that not all things will come to me in my time.....many times the understanding of things will come to me in their own time."

Great Ben continued "And your job in the meantime?"

"Well....I certainly must continue to make chalices.....I must finish the ones I started that are back at the cave.....the ones for my parents and the one for Allura Rose."

Great Ben smiled. "Good enough answer for now. Now please accept this."

Great Ben pulled out of his cloth sack a chalice. It was not any chalice though. It was the most beautiful chalice Palryma had ever seen. It was encrusted in tiny rubies and diamonds.... hundreds of them. It shone so brightly in the Matra-Matoo sun that Bird covered his eyes with his wings.

"What is that on the inside of the cup?" asked Youngie.

"Gold" said Great Ben matter-of-factly. "When I was a very young chalice maker, all the chalices were lined with gold on the inside. It was a common practice. I have even made a few that were crafted completely from gold. All the gold in the land came from Latima until bandits came in and corrupted its use. I think it was around the time of the reign of Hurrah the Beloved. It seems so long ago now and Latima has never been the same since the bandits arrived. It gets worse and worse every year. Quite a shame, too. It used to be such a beautiful place — almost as beautiful as Matra-Matoo."

"It's so shiny that I can see myself in it." exclaimed Bird.

"Not a very accurate reflection is it, Bird?" said Great Ben. "It's a bit distorted. Gold does that to everything....distorts it, that is. Very pretty to look at though."

"Great Ben...I cannot accept this. It is too much....way too precious."

"Nonsense.....it's not precious at all....what is precious to me is your friendship. I want you to present this to your love......use it at your marriage celebration....if, she accepts that is!" he said with a wink.

"I don't know how to thank you. I am sure Allura Rose will love it."

"That's all that matters." said Great Ben.

Palryma held the chalice up to have a better look at it. "What is this on the base...some writing?"

"Oh...yes....this is one of the very first chalices I made and my guide told me something very important so I inscribed it into the base of the chalice.....so I would not ever forget it. Now I pass it on to you."

Palryma inspected the inscription on the base more closely. *"Ekta laroo sora nite mu gara".* "What does that mean?" he asked.

The old wizened chalice maker looked into the violet eyes of the young chalice maker standing before him. "You will know in time, Palryma. It will be shown to you by and by... perhaps sooner than you think."

Palryma hopped on Youngie's back. "Then I will be

patient and wait for it to be revealed!"

With that and several strong flaps of his golden wings, Youngie lifted himself and his passengers up into the Matra-Matoo sky. Palryma waved to Great Ben standing below and the master waved back.

"Good-bye Great Ben!" yelled Bird "We will see you soon!"

As time passed and they made the long flight over the great lake on their way back home everyone was, again, unusually silent until Youngie spoke. "This is such a beautiful lake. I don't remember it being so beautiful when we were on our way to Great Ben's."

"A lot of things seem different to me now after my visit with Great Ben. How about you, Bird?"

"I am still Bird!" he said "I liked the blue colored too-too-too berries the best and Great Ben is very nice. I hope we come back here again."

Palryma nodded. "Yes...I think another trip here is definitely in order."

"Maybe he will give you another chalice!" said Bird.

"I think the one I hold in my hand is more than enough." Palryma said as he looked at it again. What he saw on the base of the chalice almost caused him to fall off of Youngie's back. "Sweet Lenora-ga!" he whispered.

"Sweet Lenora-ga! I can't believe it! Hello and heavens above to everyone!!!"

"What is it, Sir?!" shouted Bird "Is something the matter?"

"Not at all, Bird!!! Not at all, my fine friend! Everything is right! I understand now. I understand!!"

Neither Youngie nor Bird knew what had come over the young chalice maker.

Palryma gabbed the chalice tightly in his hand and raised his arms way above his head.

"Woo-hoo!!" he yelped "Take us home, Youngie! Take us home as fast as you can!"

The original inscription on the base of the chalice had disappeared. In its place was this:

THE JOB OF THE CHALICE MAKER IS TO LOVE

The End

Made in the USA
Middletown, DE
05 March 2018